ABBY RUSSEL

SHE WALKS
WITH SHADOWS

TITLETOWN
PUBLISHING

SHE WALKS
WITH SHADOWS

TitleTown Publishing, LLC
P.O. Box 12093 Green Bay, WI 54307-12093
920.737.8051 | titletownpublishing.com

Cover Designer: Erika L. Block
Editor: Cassidy Schwimmer
Copy Editor: Megan Richard

Author Photo: kaseyandben.com

PUBLISHER'S CATALOGING-IN-PUBLICATION DATA:

Names: Russel, Abby, author.
Title: She walks with shadows / Abby Russel.
Description: Green Bay, WI : TitleTown Publishing, LLC, [2022] Identifiers: ISBN: 978-1-955047-12-8 (paperback) 978-1-955047-61-6 (eBook)
Subjects: LCSH: Teenage girls--Fiction. | Psychic ability--Fiction. | Friendship--Fiction. | Swindlers and swindling--Fiction. | Revenge--Fiction. | Bildungsromans, American. | Self-acceptance--Fiction. | LCGFT: Paranormal fiction. | Ghost stories. | Bildungsromans. | Romance fiction.

Abby Russel is a student at St. Norbert College, where she began studying at 16 years old. She is a dancer trained in ballet, contemporary, and jazz, and now teaches at a local studio in Green Bay, WI. In her nonexistent spare time, Abby enjoys playing with her dog Gidget and listening to records. She hopes to continue writing and pursue a career with the performing arts in the future.

TABLE OF CONTENTS

1

A GIRL AND SOME GHOSTS

It wasn't always dark when the spirits came. In movies, they drifted in the darkness of the witching hour. True, sometimes they showed up at Lou's bedside, waking her at three in the morning with a cool breeze, but most often they came in broad daylight, watching her from a distance or sitting across from her at the breakfast table. As long as seventeen-year-old Lou Brightly could remember, she had seen ghosts.

She could tell when they were coming. The air around her would feel suddenly chilled and wet. A shudder would race down her spine. Sometimes they even had a distinct smell. But as of late, Lou developed an early warning system through Sunny, her young chocolate lab. Whenever Sunny's ears perked, Lou braced herself for whatever soul had decided to visit her. Not that there weren't regulars. A small girl with rosy cheeks and a bright smile would whisper a sweet *good morning* to Lou. A man with a droopy face, yellow raincoat, and a fishing pole liked to show up when it was cloudy. Lou didn't have favorites, but she was particularly fond of an old, hunched woman who had kindness in her eyes.

Despite the hauntings, Lou was content enough. She lived only a few miles away from Laguna Beach in a tiny yellow house at the bottom of a steep concrete driveway. The house possessed a certain charm, but you could barely see it from the road. Perhaps it was a good thing they had few visitors, for the house always reeked of lavender essential oils. Her mother Myra was a yoga instructor and a firm believer in all things natural and spiritual. Lou's father was out of the picture, but she didn't miss him much. Myra often harped about how her father did more spiritual damage to her than twenty years of running a business. Just as well. Lou lived happily with her mother and Sunny, and she liked it just the way it was.

She would have liked to have some friends, though. She didn't have any. Not in the way most teenagers didn't have any. When other kids her age said that they didn't have friends it meant that they had a small friend group that they didn't like very much. Lou had *zero*. While she tried to conceal her gift, it always came out in the end because of an unfortunate documentary. A local news station broadcasted about her and her gift when she was seven. No one wanted to be friends with *ghost girl* after that.

Not that she didn't *try* to make friends. But circumstances set her up to fail every time she bothered to say "hello" to another kid her age. She and her mother lived in a wealthier area of Orange County because it was good for business. The extraordinarily wealthy could afford Myra's yoga classes. But the kids of the extraordinarily wealthy wouldn't stoop so low as to be friends with Lou. Their parents would probably forbid them anyway. Lou ached for a chance, *just one chance*, to be normal. A chance to be liked. A chance to go out and do normal things without being harassed by her past—or her present.

It was a seemingly normal day in June. Sunny snored next to Lou in a bed that was too small for one person, much less for one person and a dog. Around eight the little girl, with her sparkling smile, appeared and whispered *good morning*. Lou stirred, threw on some clothes, and went to the delicate blue kitchen to make coffee. Sunny trailed behind her. She passed her mother in the living room who sat criss-crossed on a yoga mat in deep meditation. Strong incense burned next to her, making Lou's head feel foggy.

In the kitchen, Lou rearranged a few healing crystals out of the way of her favorite mug. One of her mother's eccentricities was her beloved crystal collection and the house was scattered with them for optimal *spiritual healing*. Lou poured her coffee, the only sound radiating from the room was the slow drizzle into the cup. She was disturbed from her daily routine when she felt Sunny gently bump her nose into the back of her leg. The hairs on her arms prickled, and she looked to her left to find that the old woman had come to see her. To Lou, the woman looked as real as any other living person. Wrinkles ran deep around her eyes. A gray shawl covered her shoulders. Lou caught the familiar scent of cat hair and caramel. She sipped her coffee and waved. The old woman just smiled.

"Who is it?"

Lou spun to see that her mother had crept up behind her. She had seen Lou wave.

"The old woman," she answered.

Myra followed Lou's gaze, but of course, she could see nothing. "You should give her a name."

Lou raised the question with her brows to the old woman who shook her head disapprovingly.

"She doesn't want one," Lou said. When she looked back, the old woman had gone.

Her mother just *hmm*'ed and sat down at the kitchen table where she leafed through a newspaper. Lou watched her in silent admiration. Her mother was beautiful. Myra's blonde corkscrew curls were pulled back, a strand or two popping out to frame her face. Her light eyes possessed a certain glow as they scanned the headlines. Lou thought it must be difficult for her mom that Lou had all of the traits of her father: brown hair, freckles, and hazel eyes. A reminder. Lou ruffled her own hair, which she had cut to her chin, and straightened her bangs insecurely.

Myra read the paper every morning. Lou was pretty sure she was the only person under eighty-five that still read it, but it was just another beloved eccentricity of her mother's. Her mother looked at it with a particular intensity this morning, one eyebrow raised high above the other.

"Good cartoon?" Lou joked and sipped her coffee.

"Har-har," Myra said, and then spread the paper out with her hands on the kitchen table. "You know Miles Dayholt?"

Silly question. Of course she knew who Miles Dayholt was. The Dayholt family was something of a legend in Orange County.

Miles Dayholt was one of the wealthiest men on the west coast, and he made the news biweekly for whatever rich man stunt he pulled. *Miles Dayholt Donates a Three-Million-Dollar Helicopter.* Whatever the headline, there was always an air of mystery behind it. There were very few pictures of Miles, and he was always wearing sunglasses. It was said he had a wife and kids, but nobody had ever seen them. *The Dayholt's: California's Most Private Family.* It was as if they lived on a cloud, and the only proof of their existence was found in the millions of dollars Miles chucked down like expensive hail.

"What now?" Lou asked.

Myra pointed at the paper. *Dayholt Donates One Million Dollars to the Community,* Lou read.

"So?" Lou didn't see anything unusual about this.

"Can you imagine having that much money?" her mother said, turning to the next page. "That must have quite a negative effect on his spirituality."

"Mm-hm," Lou said. She could care less about Mr. Dayholt's spirituality. "I'm going to walk Sunny."

"Have you eaten yet today?"

Dammit, she thought. Lou rubbed her eyes with the backs of her hands. "I had coffee."

"Coffee?" Said her mother, unimpressed.

"It's what the universe wanted me to have for breakfast this morning," Lou quipped over her shoulder as she turned to leave. "You always say not to mess with the universe."

Her mother sighed. Lou stood and waited for what was coming next.

"Watch for boys," her mother said absentmindedly. "They're scoundrels."

Ah, her mother's favorite mantra. It probably had to do with the way things ended with her father. Lou never bothered to question it. If there was one thing she learned from her seventeen years on earth, it was that her mother was usually...*usually* right.

Sunny, eager for her walk, wagged her tail.

• • •

Lou breathed in the golden scent of the California sun. The water was just visible from her house, a serene crescent of turquoise on the horizon. Palm trees rustled in the sweet wind. Neighbors were only a few short steps away on either side of their house, and Lou heard them stirring in their houses, marking the beginning of a new morning. She and Sunny gripped the pavement as they climbed up the sloped driveway. Sunny's paws clicked on the sidewalk as she trotted happily along, remaining only a few inches away from Lou's side. Lou never found it necessary to leash Sunny. She was strikingly intuitive, always seeming to understand Lou even more than her own mother. Sunny looked up at her, copper eyes wide and tongue out. Lou smiled. *Forget humans. You're my best friend,* she thought.

Like some kind of cruel joke, she never expected Sunny to *immediately* run forward.

Sunny stopped as suddenly as she started, several feet away. Her tail was high and ears perked. "What?" Lou asked, and she tried to see what Sunny was looking at. She couldn't see anything that Sunny would be interested in.

And then she bolted.

Lou's stomach dropped to her toes. She watched with horror and disbelief as Sunny streaked across the road.

"Sunny!"

Lou took off, legs burning as she pounded down the pavement. Sunny disappeared into someone's hedges and Lou tripped over her own feet as she ran to the adjoining road, hoping she would meet Sunny on the other side.

But there was nothing.

Lou's heart thrummed in her ears. There were other morning walkers on the sidewalk. "Have you seen my dog?" She frantically approached every stranger, who either responded with a cold "No" or shook their heads, bewildered. "Have you seen a brown lab? With a yellow collar?" With every denial, Lou's heart beat hotter and faster. Her eyes felt suddenly wet. *Don't cry,* she thought. *Crying won't get Sunny back.* She hurtled to a different road. It was empty.

Time seemed to stop, and the once beautiful palm trees looked menacing as they closed in around her. This couldn't be happening. Sunny didn't just run off. This had to be a dream. It *had* to be. She patted her pockets for her phone, but an image of it beside her bed plugged into its charger flashed in her mind.

Lou allowed herself a particularly nasty swear word to escape her lips.

She read the street sign: *Waterloo Drive.* She wasn't far from home. Maybe she could go back to the house, get her phone, or—

But then she saw something very unusual.

Up ahead, Sunny sped towards her in the passenger seat of a gleaming silver BMW convertible. Her front paws were perched on top of the passenger seat door, tail wagging enthusiastically, tongue flapping wildly in the wind. Once she processed what she saw, Lou leapt and waved her hands above her head. "That's my dog!" she shouted. The BMW slowed and signaled that it was about to pull over.

Relief flooded down Lou's body like icy water.

Now that it was closer, Lou studied the car's passengers. Her stomach did a funny flip flop. Two teenage boys occupied the convertible. The driver immediately gave Lou an impression of assertiveness and a good handshake. He sat comfortably in the driver's seat with one hand lazily set on the steering wheel. He wasn't hard on the eyes. He was the kind of person Lou's mother would describe as having "good bone structure." Designer sunglasses sat on his straight nose making him look authoritative. His sandy hair was windblown, yet it still managed to look perfectly *tousled.* In the backseat sat another boy, this one more delicate and refined looking. He too wore sunglasses; except the way he wore them reminded Lou of a model for an expensive Italian company. His brown curls grazed his forehead and framed his high cheekbones. Lou wondered if hair that remained perfectly disheveled came with an abundance of money, which these boys certainly had.

Sandy-haired Mr. Enterprise killed the engine. He leaned forward so he could see behind Sunny in the passenger seat, who looked very satisfied with herself.

"This your dog?"

Lou blinked and then remembered why she was talking to them. "Yes!" She tried to control her voice, which quivered. "Where'd you find her?" She could swear Sunny was smiling.

"She was wandering in the street," Mr. Enterprise said. "Picked her up and decided to drive around to see if the owner was nearby." He nodded towards Lou, "And they were." He smiled, flashing two rows of perfect white teeth.

Sunny jumped out of the car and joined Lou on the sidewalk. She settled at her side, panting in the hot sun.

"Thank you," Lou said.

Mr. Enterprise waved a hand dismissively, as if it had been nothing.

"No really," Lou insisted. "I was super worried."

Model-boy in the backseat muttered something and Mr. Enterprise tilted his head to listen. He frowned, then murmured something back to model-boy. All the while, they seemed to be glancing back and forth from each other and then to Lou. It greatly bothered Lou that with the sunglasses, she couldn't tell where they were looking. She fidgeted uncomfortably, looping her finger in Sunny's collar. She was suddenly very aware of the shorts she was wearing, which she had modified by ripping the seams from the bottom and running them over with her mother's car for an effect she called *distressing*. Finally, the boys seemed to have come to a consensus. Mr. Enterprise cleared his throat.

"What's your name?"

"Lou."

"Is that short for Louise or something?"

She frowned. "Not the last time I checked."

Mr. Enterprise chuckled, but Lou didn't think she had said anything funny. He outstretched his hand. "I'm Hayes."

Reluctantly, Lou stepped forward. She tried to recall how many boys her age introduced themselves with a cordial handshake. She couldn't think of one. His hand was strong and warm, which confirmed her suspicions: good handshake.

"Back here is Cleo," he gestured with his head at model boy, who held up a shy wave.

Lou smiled politely, but she checked herself and remembered her mother's philosophy. *No boys. They're scoundrels.* She couldn't imagine what her mother would say about these boys who sped around with their BMW, perfect smiles, and pockets so deep that they could spend frivolously. Lou was accustomed to seeing wealth in her area, and she knew the type.

"Thanks again," Lou said, stepping back from the convertible.

Mr. Enterprise furrowed his brow.

"Hold on. We were just going to ask if you wanted to go hiking with us sometime. We've been meaning to go but we need a third-party member."

Lou eyed him skeptically.

"...We start arguing." He looked back at model-boy, who nodded in agreement. Mr. Enterprise studied Lou's uncertain expression and then he added, "We have a private hiking trail. You can bring your dog," he said.

Sunny peered up at Lou expectantly, who shifted uncomfortably. *They have a private hiking trail?* Of course they did. Her heart fluttered. This was her chance to be normal. It was just an innocent hike with a couple of boys who never had to know about her second sight. Hell, they'd probably forget her name by the time the hike was over. But her mother's singsong voice echoed in her head. *Boys are scoundrels.*

In her peripherals, Lou could see that the old woman had returned. Lou allowed herself a quick glance and she saw that she was smiling and pointing at the boys encouragingly.

Lou laughed nervously. "O-K." She paused in between each letter.

Mr. Enterprise grinned. "Fantastic!" He rummaged through the glovebox and offered Lou a pen and a crumpled receipt. "I'll text you?" He seemed eager.

She took the pen and scrawled her number on the back. She

tried not to think about what purchase was recorded on the other side.

"There you go," she said, trying to keep her voice even while she handed the pen and receipt back to Mr. Enterprise. Model-boy beamed in the backseat. At least those two seemed happy about recent developments.

"Shall I give you a ride back home?" Mr. Enterprise asked.

"No," Lou said all too quickly, thinking about how their tiny yellow house would be the punch line of a bad joke to these boys. "Sunny and I can manage."

"Alright," he put the receipt in his breast pocket. "Nice to meet you, Sunny," he said, looking down at Sunny, who wagged. "You too, Lou" he pulled his sunglasses forward just enough so Lou could see his crystal blue eyes which somehow made him infinitely more attractive, which Lou hadn't thought was possible.

The tips of her ears burned.

"See ya," she said.

"Take care," Mr. Enterprise turned the key and the engine of the BMW roared to life. Model-boy waved enthusiastically as the engine revved, and the convertible pulled out into the street, speeding off with incredible noise and power.

Lou was frozen on the hot sidewalk. She had just given her number to two boys. Two incredibly good-looking boys in a luxury convertible. What had this day come to? What would her mother say? She would worry about that later.

The old woman appeared at Lou's side.

"Why I listen to you, I don't know," Lou sighed with exasperation at the old woman who smiled sweetly back at her, eyes crinkled in the corners.

Sunny's tail was a blur as it thumped against the pavement.

"You too, Sunny. It's almost like you both planned for this."

Sunny's tail just thumped harder.

2

MR. ENTERPRISE

Hayes was in a very good mood. As the BMW wound up the open drive that curved round a tight slope, he grinned. The breeze roared in his ears. The BMW roared beneath him. The base throbbed to a song from The Human League. Cleo sat in the back, tilting his head back to look at the azure sky. What a morning. Hayes had just gotten a number from a very pretty girl.

Well...it had been a group effort.

The dog had been sitting serenely in the middle of the road as if she had been *waiting* for them. Her tail was little more than a brown blur as it thumped against the pavement. After collecting the dog and driving around, the boys saw the girl on the sidewalk with her hands waving frantically above her head.

Hayes had never seen someone so dainty...yet *edgy*. Lou's brown hair blew in delicate wisps across her cheeks, making her look sweet and supple, yet her ripped shorts and probing gaze said *tortured soul*. There was something in the air around her that felt ethereal, magical. There was a cool breeze and a flowery scent which seemed to be distinct to her. Was it lavender? Either way, neither of the boys could disregard the way that their hearts thrummed in their chests, a heavy metronome in their ears. It was Cleo's idea to ask her to go hiking. A genius move.

The wind rustled through the palm trees and the BMW climbed the rest of the slope with a series of mechanical growls and gurgles. It wasn't that Hayes went fast. Well, he went a little fast. But the main problem with Hayes' driving was that he hadn't the faintest idea how to drive stick. The tires squealed across the pavement, and Cleo felt his stomach drop.

"Still on for pictures?" Hayes asked.

"Sure," Cleo winced as Hayes took a turn a bit too sharply. At least he signaled.

"Later we should text Lou," Hayes said. "Good idea with the hiking."

"Your parents aren't going to like this."

Hayes grinned wildly. "I don't care anymore. I should get to decide who I surround myself with." His parents had a beautifully rose-colored idea in their head about the type of man they wanted Hayes to be; a serious and sophisticated businessman, not a *photographer*. They wanted him to go to college, not *travel*. They probably wouldn't want them hanging out with someone like Lou, either. Hayes could picture his father saying how it would be *bad for his painstakingly cultivated image* to spend time with a girl who wore mutilated shorts. Screw status. Hayes had liked her shorts. He wasn't going to wait for his parents' approval. Not for this. Not anymore.

So many burdens came with being a Dayholt.

"You know that they sell automatic BMWs, right?" Cleo gritted his teeth and clutched the headrest in front of him as Hayes made a sloppy gear shift.

"It's more fun this way!" Hayes shouted over the engine.

"I'm just not sure you know what you're do— "

Cleo didn't get to finish his sentence because Hayes jammed on the brakes so hard that Cleo had to *brace himself against the back of the passenger seat* to stop his head from hitting the dashboard.

Cleo gritted his teeth. "What the hell, man?"

"Sorry. That red light came out of nowhere."

• • •

Don't think about them. They're not going to text you. When Lou and Sunny returned home from their eventful walk, she told herself that she would likely never hear from the boys again. After all, her mother had spent the entirety of Lou's life touting that boys were *scoundrels,* and Lou believed it. Nonetheless, she still checked her cracked iPhone 6 every other minute for notifications. The only messages, however, were a plethora of junk emails and a text from her mom that said "Gone shopping. Remember to eat lunch!" She sighed and set her phone down on the bedside table with a *ca-thunk.*

She agonized over her mother's second text. "Remember to eat lunch," which was a polite translation for "If you don't eat lunch, prepare for a shit-storm." Lou hadn't meant to develop an eating disorder. But then again, no one ever means to. Between her ghostly companions making more frequent and lengthier appearances and her senior year of high school quickly approaching, it just happened. It started slowly, and then came in full force. Restrict, restrict, control, control. It felt the same. In a life in which she had little control, she fought for every last bit of it. She wanted someone to tell her that there was more to life than an unstable battle for control, but it felt necessary for her survival in a world where she had been handed a scarlet letter.

The whole documentary business.

The Girl Who Walks with Shadows, it had been called. The documentary aired when Lou was seven, and it featured a wide-eyed and freckled young Lou talking to different specialists of the paranormal, one of which happened to be her father. Her mother had trusted her father, and he used her daughter for *clout.* Now the documentary had over ten million views on YouTube. She was the "ghost girl."

Lou sulked to the kitchen where she ate Frosted Cheerios from the box. Sunny stared at her feet hoping for a few fallen pieces. Outside, clouds blew across the sun and the man in the yellow raincoat clumped across the kitchen tiles with a face so miserable that it made Lou look absolutely merry by comparison.

"Catch anything?" Lou asked.

The man slammed his fishing pole to the ground and glowered.

Lou held up her hand defensively, releasing some Cheerios to the delight of Sunny. After stomping around for a minute, the man and his fishing pole evaporated.

In the next room, her phone vibrated.

In her haste to retrieve it, the neglected box of cereal knocked over. Sunny quickly licked up the spilled circles as Lou returned to the kitchen.

"Hey. Enough cereal for you." Lou snatched the box away and set it upright on the kitchen table. She gathered the courage to check her phone and quickly flicked it on.

Sure enough, she had a new text message from a number that wasn't programmed into her phone yet.

"Hey Lou. It's Hayes," the text said.

Lou pretended she had been aloof. "Oh yeah," she typed, "Hey there." Right after she hit send, she received another text.

"Still on for hiking?"

Lou smiled. So he had been serious. She felt giddy, but there was no way she was going to let Mr. Enterprise know that.

"Sure," she said.

"Fantastic," he said, and Lou could picture his winning grin. "Tomorrow?"

Her heart stopped. Tomorrow was very close. She considered this. Where would her mother be? Yoga. Myra taught three classes, which would give her a span of at least four to five hours.

"Tomorrow is good," she said, hitting *send* with gusto.

"Excellent," he replied, still just as quickly as before. "Where do you want me and Cleo to pick you up?"

Lou's fingers flew across her phone screen as she thought of all the possible ways to say *not here.* Not her lavender-reeking, crystal strewn yellow house. Finally, she decided on "Waterloo Drive." After all, it had been the first place they'd met.

"Perfect."

Lou was astounded at how many variations of the word "good" Mr. Enterprise had.

"9 am. Be there or be square," he said.

Lou didn't send anything else except a yellow smiley.

Her mind raced with excitement. Tomorrow felt like the start of something new. Maybe boys weren't all scoundrels. Maybe these boys would help her get what she had longed for: a sense of normality. Friends.

Lou made a vow that Hayes and Cleo were *never* going to find out about her ghosts.

She wasn't going to mess this up.

3

MOTHERS ALWAYS KNOW

On the morning of the hike, Lou made sure to be on good terms with her mother—but not so good that it would raise suspicion. *Act normal. Be natural. Play it cool.* She got up, made her tiny bed, and turned the kettle on for Myra's tea.

"I should be home around two," said Myra, who was getting creative with the way she rolled her yoga mat so that it would fit in her bag.

"Okay," Lou said, making a bold mental note. *Two o'clock.*

"Love you, sunshine." Lou didn't duck as she usually did when her mother went in to kiss her forehead. "I'll see you later."

"Later," Lou smiled sweetly.

Their house was so small that when she closed the door, the walls quivered ever so slightly. Lou watched from the window as her mom's black Honda Civic ascended the steep driveway and pulled out into the street.

"It's hiking time!" Lou jumped high into the air. Sunny barked excitedly.

After a nerve-wracking walk, the pair made it to Waterloo Drive. Sunny ran circles around Lou's feet as she scanned the area for the silver BMW.

After what seemed like forever, she watched as it finally pulled up next to the curb. Her heart lifted in her chest. A small, albeit foolish, part of her hadn't expected them to show up. But they had. Mr. Enterprise and Model-boy waved when they saw her. Sunny waved her signature greeting, wagging her tail furiously against the ground.

Cleo scurried out of the passenger seat and held the door for Lou. Even in his Hawaiian patterned shirt, he managed to look elegant. With the absence of his sunglasses, Lou could see his eyes for the first time, which were a rich honey brown. Compared to the rest of him, his eyes were distinctively boyish.

"Thanks," Lou said, as she slid into the convertible. Of all the places she envisioned herself, she never imagined that she would be sitting in a BMW. The seats themselves looked more expensive than her house.

"Always prefer the back when he drives, anyway," Cleo said quietly. Lou realized this was the first time she had heard him talk. His voice was also boyish. He and Sunny jumped into the back, and Lou thought that they looked awfully similar as they sat side by side with wide, giddy smiles.

"Ready, Lou?" Mr. Enterprise asked. He sat coolly in the driver's seat; one hand set idly on the steering wheel as it had been the day before. His alluring eyes were the same penetrating blue.

Lou tried her best not to flush red.

"Ready," she said, stopping herself from slipping into her habit of adjusting her bangs.

Hayes bent to the side and retrieved a cardboard drink carrier with three massive Starbucks cups in it.

"You drink coffee?" he asked, but he was already handing her one of the giant travel cups.

"Thank you," she said, and she sipped it.

Cream.

Too many calories.

Lou brushed off the rising feeling of unease. She refused to let a little bit of cream ruin her day. She just hoped none of her apparitions would pay her a visit.

"Right," Hayes handed Cleo his drink and then chucked the drink carrier behind his seat, "Let's go." The engine revved, and Lou felt herself jolt into the back of her seat.

Lou remembered what Cleo had said. *Always prefer the back when he drives.* Now she knew why. The car hurtled into the warm air of the California morning. Every time Hayes fumbled with the gear shift, Lou felt a knot tighten in her stomach. In all aspects, cunning Mr. Enterprise seemed to be the kind of person who knew what he was doing. But from where Lou sat, tightening her seatbelt, she felt that maybe he didn't know much when it came to driving stick.

She looked back at her dog, who had her tongue out in typical Sunny fashion, eyes closed and content as she took in all of the luscious scents of the palms and ocean nearby. At least Sunny was happy. Cleo winced as flying pieces of dog hair cascaded into his face.

"How's your morning?" Hayes asked Lou nonchalantly, clearly not as concerned as anyone else about his driving capabilities.

"Good," Lou swallowed, trying to level her voice so it didn't sound as nervous as she felt. She sipped her cream-corrupted coffee.

Mr. Enterprise had obviously been looking for more of an answer than *good*.

"Do anything interesting?"

"Does this count?" Lou asked.

Hayes grinned his champion smile.

"Sure. You like hiking?"

"Never been," Lou answered honestly. "Not unless you count walking up and down Sunset Boulevard."

Mr. Enterprise chuckled.

"No, not quite the same thing. Today you're going to experience the thrill of the woods."

Lou couldn't imagine there being any *woods* in suburban California, but she went along with it.

"Where's the trail?" she asked.

"Just up in Temple Hills. A few miles ahead of where I live, actually. My family owns the trail—I think I told you that," he said it as if it was perfectly ordinary to own a section of woods reserved for personal use.

"I think you mentioned it," she said.

"Just so you know, there probably won't be cell service," Cleo interjected from the back.

"That's okay," Lou said. It didn't matter. As long as she was back by two, there shouldn't be any problems.

In hindsight, she wished she had been more careful with her blissful teenage naivety.

• • •

The start of the trail sloped into the embrace of the trees at the base of Temple Hills. Lou hadn't seen so much green in one place for a long time. Hayes jerked the BMW to a stop a few yards from the mouth of the well-kept path. Lou stepped dreamily out of the car taking in the rustic scenery. She couldn't decide if the air was warm or cool. It was just right. She had been wrong to doubt Hayes. These were *woods,* no question. A fragrant breeze stirred the forest in a chorus of leafy whispers, and the sun beat down its golden light. Sunny was out and sniffing the ground fervently, zigzagging this way and that as she caught a new scent.

"Wow," Lou breathed, "It's beautiful."

Cleo and Hayes stood side by side with their hands on their hips in a manner that suggested that they were satisfied. This was the reaction they had hoped for.

"Shall we go in?" Hayes asked.

Strands of sunlight streamed down from the canopy of leaves as the trio trekked along the dirt path. Sunny wasn't too far up ahead. She was easily spotted by her tail that wagged a million miles an hour. Lou walked in a trance-like state, feeling slightly euphoric as she took in all of the greenery.

Hayes slapped at a gnat that landed on his arm.

"So Lou, what do you do?"

"Huh?" The question startled her.

"You know—when you're not hiking with two extraordinarily average guys who rescued your dog. What do you do?"

Extraordinarily average? Lou thought. Modesty did not become

Mr. Enterprise with his bright smile, luxury convertible, and his ability to remain effortlessly deft and charming. But she had other concerns. What *did* she do? She couldn't exactly say "Oh, you know, I talk to ghosts and restrict my caloric intake." Lou was beginning to realize that she was extraordinarily boring, besides of course the ghost aspect, but there was no way she was going to talk about *that*.

Finally, she said, "I like to draw." She wasn't sure if her mess of charcoal smears and scribbles counted as drawing, but it was better than the alternative.

"Neat," Hayes said, "What do you draw?" To her surprise, it sounded as though his interest was genuine.

"I guess it's...abstract?" Before he could say anything else, she asked, "What about you?"

"Photography," Hayes said, holding up the camera that hung around his neck. Lou hadn't noticed it before. "Much to my parent's distaste."

Lou could imagine. Whoever Hayes' parents were, it was clear that they were wealthy, maybe even powerful. She was sure that they had high expectations of him growing up to become an aristocrat.

"What do you take pictures of?"

"Mostly nature. And Cleo," he grinned.

Cleo made a noise in the back of his throat.

For a minute, Lou had forgotten Cleo was there. There was an interesting dynamic between him and Mr. Enterprise. Where Hayes was self-assured and sociable, Cleo was reserved, shy even. The difference was astounding. Lou remembered when they had first invited her along: *We need a third-party member...we start arguing.* She couldn't imagine what these two would fight about.

They stopped at a crest overlooking the water. The waves crashed into the rocky shoreline and blew salt through their hair. Hayes stood with his camera pointed at the ocean and its blueness. Lou was adjusting Sunny's collar. Cleo just watched. He tried to be smooth as he gulped from his water bottle, but he ended up missing his mouth completely and slurped water all over his shirt. Cleo tried to clean himself up the best he could before Lou noticed.

Lou was enchanted by the morning she was having. She had forgotten about the milky coffee. And her ghosts. She was just *being. Existing.* And most importantly, *enjoying a hike with two very attractive boys.*

"Thank you for bringing me here," Lou said.

"Don't mention it," Hayes smiled as he jumped down from the rock. "Do you mind?" he asked, pointing from his camera to Lou.

She blushed.

"Okay," she moved in front of the view of the water. Suddenly, she didn't know what to do with her arms, her legs, her face…or anything. She had chosen a simple white Champion tee and black athletic shorts, a significantly less shaggy option compared to her distressed short outfit, but still less than ideal.

To make matters worse, a new spirit materialized in front of her. It was an old man with a red baseball cap. He looked confused. The new ones always did. His neck sunk into his shoulders, and he looked at Lou expectantly, waiting for her to explain to him why he was here. But Lou didn't say anything. After all, what could she say?

Focus, Lou thought.

"What do I do?" she turned her attention back to posing for the picture, which was arguably more upsetting than the apparition.

Hayes smiled reassuringly.

"Just be you." With that, he put the camera in focus and took the picture with a soft *click.*

At 1:50, the boys dropped Lou and Sunny off on Waterloo Drive. Sunny stretched contentedly on the sidewalk.

"We should do this again," Hayes said.

"Yeah, sure. Okay." she tried to sound excited enough but not *too* excited. She didn't want to come off as desperate for their company, even if she was.

"Is it okay if I make a group chat with Cleo in it?" Hayes asked as he coolly raised his sunglasses down to look her in the eyes. She could have melted.

"Sure," Lou tore her attention away long enough to smile at Cleo, who was suddenly very interested in picking an invisible piece of lint off his shirt.

"See you," she grinned and waved.

"See you," the boys echoed at the same time.

The convertible revved, and she laughed when Hayes made a terrible gear shift as he sped off down the street.

Lou's heart soared the entire way home. Sunny had to trot to keep up with the extra pep in her step.

For the first time since Lou was seven, friendship didn't seem so far out of reach.

● ● ●

When she made it back to her little yellow house, she immediately knew something was wrong. Her mother's Honda Civic was in the driveway. The lights in the house were on.

"Shit."

She bolted inside, Sunny at her heel, the screen door clattering shut behind them.

It didn't take long for Lou to find her mother. She stopped dead in her tracks.

Myra's lips were pursed. She sat at the kitchen table, one hand folded over the other. "So," her mother said. Her voice was tight. Lou was rigid with fear. "When exactly did we start lying to each other? Hm?" Her mother tilted her head to one side, and Lou bit her lip.

"I—I— "

Her mother held out her palm in front of her face.

"Don't. No more lies. If you're going to lie, don't bother saying anything."

She knows, Lou thought.

"My last two classes were cancelled today," Myra explained sharply. "When I came home to an empty house, I thought that you were out with Sunny. That was until the first hour passed. And then the second. And then the third." Her brows hung low, but her lip quivered. "Do you know how terrifying it is to come home and not know where your child is? I called you *six times*. You never answered."

Lou squeezed her eyes shut.

"I am only going to ask this once," her mother said, eyes slowly pooling with tears, "Where were you?"

"Mom, I'm— "

"Where were you?" She repeated.

Lou looked at her feet.

"I went hiking," she said.

"Hiking?" Immediately, Myra knew that there was more to the explanation than Lou was giving.

"I wasn't alone," she admitted ashamedly.

"Who were you with?" Myra asked calmly, which was all the more unsettling.

Lou looked up and then at her feet again. She couldn't look her mother in the eyes.

"I was with two boys."

Myra exhaled loudly through her nose.

The silence which followed felt like enough for two lifetimes. *Say something,* Lou thought. *Anything.* Lou could see the wheels turning in her mother's mind. It could be a dangerous thing to break her mother's train of thought, but Lou was so uncomfortable that she sank back in her heels. She would accept her fate.

"This won't happen again," she began quietly. "I'm so sorry. I promise I won't see them again." Lou sniffled and turned to go to her room, but her mother caught her arm.

"I'm sorry," Myra said finally, "that you didn't feel comfortable enough to tell me."

Lou's heart skipped a beat. Her mom was sorry? What for?

"You should be able to make your own decisions without having to walk on eggshells around me. Hell, you're almost an adult." Myra rubbed her eyes. "I hear some of my clients talk about how their teenagers are always rebelling, sneaking around, doing drugs— "

"I don't do drugs!" Lou interjected.

"I know, I know. But the point is I never thought...that would be us." Myra dropped her hands to her side, defeated.

Lou's voice broke, "I-I just didn't want to let you down."

Her mother smiled and stroked Lou's hair.

"You haven't let me down. You've only disappointed me."

Rather than comforting Lou, it felt like a heavy rock had sunk into the bottom of her stomach. *Isn't that the same thing...* she thought

"So," Myra clapped her hands together, now cheery and full of life. "Tell me about these boys!"

4

A BAD MAN

Miles Dayholt hated hotel rooms. They always made him feel confined, like he didn't have any room to breathe. He ran a hand through his thin, balding hair as he assessed the situation, his suitcase resting at his feet. *Yep,* he thought. He still hated hotel rooms. Even ones in Bali.

But no matter the situation, Miles Dayholt had work to do, and when he had work to do, he would stop at nothing to get it done. Except for maybe his blasted cellphone, which vibrated in his pocket. It was a text from his assistant, Karen.

"Front page in Laguna Beach!" it said.

Miles frowned. Of course. He had donated one million dollars on a day that he had felt particularly depressed and miserable about himself with hopes of making himself feel better. It hadn't. Why he continued to donate so religiously throughout the years was beyond him. The instant gratification only lasted so long.

There was another text from his youngest son, which he ignored. He didn't have the time or the patience for Hayes. Not now.

The hotel door slammed behind him.

He turned his head. *God,* he thought, *even the doors don't stay open.* He tried not to read too deeply into the symbolic meaning of this thought.

Unzipping his suitcase, he hopped onto the lumpy bed, retrieved his laptop, and opened his email. He scrolled past the stats, meeting reminders, and check-ins from his therapist until he found what he was looking for.

Another death threat.

He couldn't view the address that had sent the email, but this wasn't unordinary. The contents of the email? Only five words.

We know what you did.

Miles pressed the delete button without so much as a blink. He always felt better if he got what he liked to call his "menace mail" out of the way. Deleting emails was Dayholt's favorite part of his job. Then he would begrudgingly begin his *real* work.

Whenever someone asked Miles what he did for a living, he would maintain his signature deadpan expression and say, "I'm a con-artist." This was always reciprocated with howls of laughter, and it was one of his favorite things to do at benefit dinners and parties. *Jokes on them,* he thought.

He felt a cool breeze drift across the room. Annoyedly, he got up to close the window, which he hadn't remembered opening, but there were a lot of things Miles Dayholt couldn't remember. When he returned to his bed, his suitcase had been moved to the floor. He grunted as he flung it back on the puffed white bedspread and resumed his email-deleting business.

It was only when the lights started flicking on and off when Miles swung his legs over the side of the bed and surveyed the hotel room with acute intensity. The air was cold and damp. The only sound was a fly which beat against the window.

He felt uncomfortably feeble when he whispered, "Who's there?"

He heard the *click* of a ballpoint pen.

At the chipped hotel writing desk, an invisible hand maneuvered a pen across a notepad with the hotel's logo on it.

Miles swallowed.

The pen clattered to the floor.

On the notepad, written in craggy lettering, was a name: *Clyde Grivins.*

In a flurry, Miles stuffed his computer back into his suitcase, secured his smartphone, and pounded out of the hotel room.

He was checking out.

• • •

Myra didn't like to watch the news. It negatively impacted her spiritual well-being. But tonight it was the only thing that could keep her mind off of her troubles. Myra had been avoiding this moment her entire career as a mother; she felt like she had failed as a parent.

Maybe she had been wrong to kick her husband completely out of their lives. But then again, Lou was only a child when he *used* her for recognition.

The Girl Who Walks with Shadows.

It marked her daughter permanently. Myra wished she had been more careful. It bothered her greatly that it had happened, but what was worse, it had happened under her care.

She rubbed her temple as she squinted in the blue light of the TV. Bob Riley, the tall, clean-cut, peppy reporter was talking about a newly developed missing persons case. Myra wasn't paying a ridiculous amount of attention, but she did hear one name repeated over and over again. Clyde Grivins. Something about Bali.

Hm. Bali. She had read in the paper the other morning that Miles Dayholt was in Bali. It was the same article that announced his million-dollar donation. It's funny how people can invest so much energy into worrying about people that they've never met before.

Oh, how Myra worried about that man.

5

SECRETS

There were a few conditions in which Myra allowed Lou to continue to see Cleo and Hayes. The first was that Lou had to organize her mother's closet as punishment for being sneaky. The second was to uphold a 10 pm curfew. Lastly, much to Lou's distaste, she had to eat breakfast with her mother every morning.

"You'll run yourself into the ground if you're not careful," she said when Lou protested.

Myra did not fail twice. She was going to give her daughter some tough love.

After the slightest bit of hesitation, Lou agreed.

It was looking like it was going to be a good summer.

Lou finally allowed Hayes to pick her up at her house. Rather than disregarding the house completely like she had hoped, the boys observed it as if it was a piece of fine art.

"Look at that color," Cleo said. "It's marvelous."

Hayes closed his eyes and breathed through his nose.

"Such a nice smell. Is that lavender?"

Lou grew impatient as they talked architectural design, modernism, and Frank Lloyd Wright, all of which seemed inappropriate considering that the little yellow house was the point of discussion.

"Come on," she said, opening the door to the convertible, which looked like a great silver mosque in comparison to the house.

Her mother watched from the window as they pulled out of the driveway.

• • •

The trio had been on a plethora of adventures, and it was only the third week in June. They went to the drive-in theater, and Lou remembered wanting to be invisible as every head turned to gawk at Hayes' car. That night, the theatre featured a horror movie that had just been released. Lou had gotten a kick out of the film's interpretation of supernatural activity. As Lou snickered, Cleo struggled to maintain his composure. He was scared shitless.

On another day, Lou found herself facing one of her worst fears: a burrito. Hayes loved them, and it was his idea to stop at Chipotle for lunch after a morning at the beach.

"I'll get it," Hayes said, hopping out of the car. He had placed a mobile order fifteen minutes earlier.

Lou fiddled with her bangs.

"You know, I used to have an eating disorder, too."

She jumped. Cleo was staring at her thoughtfully.

"How did you— "

He waved a hand dismissively.

"When you've been through it, you just know." His arm rested on the door, and he looked unusually self-assured.

Lou turned sanguine.

"I don't *think* I have an eating disorder," she said. The pitch of her voice was a series of peaks and valleys. She cleared her throat. "I don't."

Cleo nodded gently, but the subtle raise of his left eyebrow spoke for him. He was not convinced.

Lou looked at her hands.

"I guess I just— "she faltered.

But Cleo didn't need an explanation.

"I'm always here if you want to talk," he said, and Lou looked back at him. It was the first time he didn't struggle to hold eye contact with her. She took all of him in, this boy with honey eyes. She felt her stomach cartwheel, and she dropped her gaze.

"I will," she smiled shyly.

What the hell is wrong with me? she thought, struggling to ignore the steady burn across her cheeks. Lou wished she had sunglasses of her own right about now.

Hayes was back far too soon, paper bags in hand. "Before you ask," he said, "*Yes, I did* get your damn red chili salsa." Cleo eagerly snatched the oil-splotched bag Hayes was holding out in front of him.

After dividing up the food, the three of them unwrapped their burritos and sprawled about the convertible.

Hayes frowned when Lou hesitated to take her first bite.

"What's wrong?" he asked, although it was barely audible through his chewing.

"Nothing," she smiled and raised the foil-wrapped burrito to her lips.

She ate it all.

It was delicious.

It had been a while since she had been so happy. She no longer flushed red when Hayes looked at her with his ever-alluring eyes. Her heart *did* continue to drum-roll in her chest, however. Additionally, she hadn't quite acclimated to his horrendous driving, but she didn't think she would ever get used to *that*. Progress was progress after all.

There was only one other unfavorable circumstance. There seemed to be a massive uptick in the number of ghosts Lou saw. She still got her *good morning* from the little ruddy-cheeked girl, periodic appointments with the old woman, and cloudy visitations from the raincoat man. However, on top of that, the red-cap man appeared for short bursts of time, a shorter man paced up and down the hallway, and a peculiar spirit which she hadn't seen any more than a shadow tapped at her window in the night. The only thing that had changed was that she had been spending more time with Cleo and Hayes, but she couldn't see how that would affect her spirits. She didn't want to think if they were connected to the increase of newcomers. They couldn't be. It made no sense.

There it was again: the teenage naivety that she normally paid an unearthly amount of attention guarding herself from was trick-ling in. Although every instinct told her not to, Lou pushed the thought to the back of her mind.

She focused instead on trying to figure out who Hayes was. She wished that she knew more about him, but he was very guarded when it came to family. Every time the conversation hovered within the vicinity of family matters; he was quick to switch the topic. Lou looked to Cleo for support, but he just shrugged. He had been loyal to Hayes for a long time, and he wasn't going to stop anytime soon.

Luckily for Lou, the answer wasn't far away.

"Where are we going?" It was another bright day in Laguna Beach, and Lou wished she had brought Sunny. She would have enjoyed the honeyed wind. The convertible gagged as Hayes made a gear change a bit too soon.

"Dude! Come on!" Cleo said from his usual place in the back. He dug his nails into the seat.

"My bad. It'll never happen again." Hayes smiled wickedly at Lou while she tried her best to hide her eye-roll from him.

The BMW climbed up a curved slope. Wherever they were going, it was much higher than sea level. The Beatles echoed through the car speakers, singing about a blackbird.

"Is it supposed to be a secret?" Lou asked, eager to get the con-versation back on track.

Hayes mulled it over for a minute, chewing on the side of his cheek, a habit of his that Lou found to be very cute.

He released his cheek. "I guess it doesn't have to be."

She raised her brows. "And?"

He didn't say anything, not until the car slowed as it approached two massive blocks of white concrete. A gate? He stopped the car and entered a lengthy password into a keypad with a little red light.

She looked back at Cleo, who smirked.

Lou hated it when he knew more than she did.

The red light flashed green.

"Home sweet home," Hayes said.

She choked.

The gate opened, revealing a mansion so colossal that *mansion* didn't seem to be a suitable enough word. It was a castle. An empire. Three pearly stories carved out the side of a hill that overlooked a desolate shoreline of the Pacific Ocean. Like the trail that they had hiked, the house was completely enclosed with luscious greenery. Even the air was fresher. Ivy crawled up the outer walls not so much that it looked overgrown, but enough to entertain the viewer. A waterfall rushed down the hill adjacent to the pool, giving the effect that the pool was the beginning of the falls. The rooms were like alcoves, jetting in and out from the main structure like a beehive. And Lou thought she knew who the queen was.

There was no other explanation.

Hayes was a Dayholt.

"Holy—," she breathed. "Y-you're a—"

"Yep." Hayes finished the word with a slight *pop*. She couldn't tell if he was nervous or agitated. Or both.

The car weaved up the smooth driveway and stopped beneath the veranda. The three sat in silence for several minutes. Lou was perplexed. How would this newfound information affect their friendship? She hoped it wouldn't. Now she knew why Hayes had been so secretive. It was for the same reason Lou had been secretive about the house she lived in. Both of them had been terrified of judgement from the other.

Hayes let it sink in before he reversed and turned the convertible back the way they came.

Cleo leaned forward to whisper in Lou's ear, "You know what this means?"

"What?" she whispered back.

"It means he trusts you."

Lou couldn't tell if this was a compliment or a warning.

Perhaps it was both.

The gates closed behind them.

6

THE MAN IN THE PHOTOGRAPH

It was just past eleven at night when Lou's phone started buzzing.

Hayes was calling her.

Under normal circumstances, she would've ignored the call completely and gone to bed—something she had been looking forward to for the past hour—but after all it was *Hayes* who was calling, and he never called.

"Hello?"

"Hey Lou."

"What's up?" She laid back in her bed and stroked Sunny's ears.

"Um..." he trailed off. She heard rustling in the background that suggested fidgeting.

Hold on. Was cool, composed Mr. Enterprise nervous?

Out of no control of her own, Lou smiled.

"Yes?" she said.

He cleared his throat.

"My brother is taking the yacht out on Saturday, and I was, uh, wondering if you wanted to come with me."

"You have a brother?"

"Yes," he said shortly, irritated that she hadn't answered his second question. "But we're not close. So, do you wanna come?"

Lou knew the right thing to do would be to answer him, but she was having too much fun taking the indirect route.

"I can't believe you didn't tell me you had a brother."

Hayes didn't even try to sound collected as he blurted, "Will you?"

She swallowed. Would she?

"Is Cleo going?"

She heard something crash on the other end of the line.

"Are you okay?"

"Fine," he answered, his voice breaking slightly. He cleared his throat before continuing, "I'm fine. Just slipped. And no. Cleo's not coming."

The scent of caramel and mothballs floated through the air, and Lou flicked her eyes to her left to see that the old woman had come. She always seemed to appear right when Hayes invited Lou somewhere. The only difference this time was that Cleo wasn't coming. They would be alone. Well, besides his brother.

The old woman smiled and winked before vanishing.

Lou brushed a strand of hair from her face.

"Is this a date?"

"Uhm…" Hayes stalled before he ripped the band-aid. "Yes."

Lou lit up.

"No flowers. I don't want any," she said coyly.

"Is that a yes?"

"That's a yes."

Relieved, he laughed, youthful and genuine.

"So you don't like flowers?"

"No, I like flowers," Lou explained. "That's why I'm asking you not to bring me any."

His confusion was disclosed by the silence at the other end of the line.

She giggled. He was bewildered.

"Flowers are killed for their beauty," she said coolly. "I prefer them when they're in the ground."

"Oh," he laughed, still giddy. "I promise no flowers."

"Okay," she said through a grin.

"I'll text you details later. See you Saturday?"

"See you Saturday."

As tired as she just was, she knew it would be the middle of the night before she finally got some rest.

• • •

Hayes hung up triumphantly. He rubbed his hands together excitedly. He had a *date*...a date with Lou! He leaned back into the swivel chair in his room with caution. He had tripped over it while he had been on the phone.

He slid over to his desktop and removed his camera's memory card. The newest pictures he had taken had finished importing. He beamed as he scrolled through the bright colors of California summer. Bright reds of flowers, rich blues of the sea, and inky purples of dusk.

Cleo would be happy, he thought as he scrolled. Hayes had a new favorite model.

There was Lou the night at the drive-in blushing red as onlookers dropped their jaws at the convertible. There was Lou throwing a red frisbee to a leaping Sunny at the beach. He had even sneakily captured her eating a burrito the day they went to Chipotle. Lou had a glow about her when she smiled into the camera. Her whole face lit up, especially her eyes which seemed to have fireflies in their irises.

For the first time in his life, Hayes thought that he might be in love.

He scrolled until the screen became a slew of green—pictures from the hiking day, and pulled up the one of Lou in front of the crest. Hayes realized it was the first picture he had taken of her. He looked at it adoringly.

And then he almost fell right out of his chair.

A picture of Lou smiling softly in front of the crest glowed on the computer monitor.

Behind her, in a red baseball cap, stood a scared-looking man.

7

LEAVE IT TO ROBERT

Lou had never been on a date before.

Just like she knew she wouldn't, she barely slept a wink. She couldn't wake her mom up in the middle of the night to tell her about it and instead forced herself to wait until morning to tell her.

"You look chipper," her mother said. She had already laid breakfast on the kitchen table, and Lou joined her. So far, she hadn't missed a single breakfast with her mother, as they had agreed upon.

Lou smiled, choosing to withhold the news for a little while longer. She poured syrup over her pancakes.

"How was class yesterday?" she asked her mom.

"It was fine," Myra said, sipping her tea. "Although it was the first class Mrs. Martinez attended since her hip replacement. She got stuck in child's pose for a little while, but we got her out of it."

Lou nodded as she chewed.

"Occupational hazard."

"Exactly," her mother said.

Lou could wait no longer. She set down her fork.

"Mom, I have something to tell you. Well—two things actually," she said, reconsidering.

"Oh?" Myra raised an eyebrow and braced herself against the table.

"You know how you're *obsessed* with the Dayholt's?" she began.

"*Pshh*," Myra rolled her eyes. "I am not obsessed. I just have a general curiosity, that's all," she said, sipping her tea.

"Okay," Lou fought the urge to smile, "Well, it turns out Hayes is Miles Dayholt's son."

Her mother choked on her tea and coughed, tears forming in her eyes as she took some water.

"Mom, are you okay?"

"Fine," she said throatily in between coughs.

"Are you ready for the second thing?"

No, no she was not.

Her mother waved a hand still wiping her red eyes, "Go on."

"Well," Lou began bashfully, "on Saturday his brother is taking out the yacht."

Oh Lord, Myra thought. Of course there was a yacht involved.

"And?"

Lou's cheeks flushed, letting the excitement build up inside of her until she couldn't hold it in any longer.

"I'm going on a date with him!" The words sprinted from her lips and she sat back in her chair all red and giggly. It was as if this one secret had her on an ultimate high, raising her up and up into the clouds until the ground was out of sight.

She watched her mother carefully, waiting for a response.

Myra sat and stared at her tea blankly. Lou knew this wasn't a good sign. *She's going to be mad,* Lou thought. Dammit. Maybe she should have left out the part about him being a Dayholt. *She's going to yell at me. Or worse, not talk to me. Or she is going to remind me that boys are scoundrels and never let me see them again.*

But only one word crossed Myra's mind.

Shit.

Her little girl had a date.

• • •

Saturday came too quickly for Hayes. He tried to shrug off what he had discovered, but he couldn't. There was, without a doubt, another person in the picture he took of Lou. He did not know the man with the red cap, and he *definitely* had not seen him on the day of the hike. After all, their hiking trail was *private.*

Regardless of what he told himself, he still texted Cleo.

"Was there anyone else on the trail the day we went hiking?"

Cleo responded with a puzzled-face emoji.

"No..." he said.

"Okay, thanks," Hayes responded quickly and turned his phone off.

Moments later it dinged again. He thought that had ended the conversation, but Cleo texted back with, "Why are you being weird?"

Hayes sighed and came up with something quick.

"Weirder than usual?"

"Good point. Never mind."

Hayes exhaled loudly and ran his hands through his hair. His date with Lou was coming up quickly. He had until then to forget about the picture. He was *not* going to mess this up.

• • •

Lou had her phone propped up on the bathroom counter. She stared into the mirror with her head tilted at an awkward angle, attempting to watch what she was doing while simultaneously following a tutorial for an updo on YouTube. Eventually she gave up. Her arms were protesting, and her hair was just too short. She gave her hair a run through with her fingers and called it good.

She only briefly considered wearing the same distressed shorts she had worn on the day they met, but quickly dismissed the idea. She decided that she ought to class it up, yet still express a little bit of herself, which meant there was going to be black involved. She chose a dark bishop-sleeved cropped blouse and jeans that resembled bell-bottoms but *were not* bell-bottoms, as she had explained to her mother.

"You look like a member of Led Zeppelin."

"Who?" Lou asked, mostly because she knew that it would annoy her. She knew exactly who her mother's favorite band was but enjoyed teasing her.

"Never mind," Myra said. "When's he coming?"

"Three," Lou said, fidgeting with her bangs.

"Or...now," said her mother absentmindedly as she pulled back the curtains and stared out the window.

Lou followed her mother's line of sight through the window to find Hayes' convertible easing down the driveway. She grabbed her bag, jammed her feet into black sandals, and opened the front door as he pulled into a jolted park.

Hayes climbed out of the convertible, sporting a light blue oxford shirt that brought out his eyes. His hair was ever-perfectly tousled. He grinned when he saw Lou and reached into the passenger seat to retrieve what looked like an empty flowerpot.

"What's that?" Lou asked.

He sauntered to the doorstep and handed it to her.

Lou could not contain her amusement, and she laughed. Hard. At the bottom of the clay pot was a packet of geranium seeds.

"No flowers were harmed in the making of this gift," he chuckled. "You can plant them sometime."

Sunny had followed Lou to the door, and she wagged when she saw Hayes. He knelt down to stroke her head. Myra had also followed. Her hands were perched firmly on her hips as she scrutinized the boy.

"Nice to finally meet you," she said, although her voice didn't sound particularly charmed.

"Oh," Hayes stood up and held out his hand. "Nice to meet you, too."

She looked at his hand incredulously and shook it.

Lou flashed her mom a warning look, but Myra flicked her eyebrows up as if to say *try me*.

"Listen," she said, boring into his eyes.

Hayes shifted uncomfortably.

"I've seen your face," she said. "I know your name."

"Mother!"

Sunny licked Hayes' hand and Myra's eyes trailed down to watch. She frowned for a minute, and Lou saw it: the wheels were turning. The last thing she said before withdrawing into the house was, "Dogs have good instincts when it comes to personality."

And then she left the two of them on the porch, satisfied that she had instilled an appropriate amount of fear.

● ● ●

Hayes offered Lou his hand as she stepped from the dock and onto the yacht, which could have fit three of Lou's houses on the deck alone. The day was sunny and clear, perfect to be out on the water, which lapped up against the side of the boat. She could see straight down to the sand that curled from the waves, and she marveled at a coastal fish that darted into the protective shadow of the yacht.

A young man who looked about twenty strode towards them, and Lou assumed this was Hayes' brother. He looked presidential as he walked towards them with rolled back shoulders and long, confident strides. Lou thought he was going to offer her a pamphlet.

"Welcome aboard," he said, shaking her hand. He raised his sunglasses which revealed that he was a slightly larger copy of Hayes, except for his eyes which were murky and brown.

"Thanks," Lou said.

"This is Robert," Hayes said shortly, eager to get the introductions over with. The less time she spent talking to his brother, the less likely Robert would inform her of something embarrassing, like the time he thought it would be funny to steal all of Hayes' underwear and line them up along the roof.

"You look familiar," he said, tapping his index finger to his chin. "I've seen you somewhere before."

Immediately her mind shot to the documentary. Surely even Dayholt's must watch documentaries.

"No," said Lou, a bit too quickly.

"What's your name?" Robert pressed.

She gulped, "Lou Brightly."

"Huh…" he sank back in his heels and stared at her for a minute, trying to place where he had seen her.

"Ugh, ignore him," Hayes said, snatching her hand. She would have taken more notice of it had her fears not completely dominated her mind.

Robert's attention snapped back to Hayes.

"She's cute," Robert said as if she wasn't there.

Lou's ears burned.

"Has he told you about his chlamydia yet?"

"Bye," Hayes said, dragging Lou behind him.

"Nice to meet you," Lou called, but it came out like *"Nice to meet you?"*

"I'll be seeing you, Brightly."

Hayes guided Lou up the stairs to the second level of the yacht. A loud rumble let Lou know that the engine had started. Shortly after, the water moved beneath them, and they were coursing out into the deeper blue.

On the second level there was a veranda with a wrap-around couch. They sat next to each other, Lou sitting awkwardly crisscrossed while Hayes sprawled out, one arm resting on the back of the couch.

"I'm sorry about my mom," Lou said, embarrassed.

He laughed, "I'm sorry about my brother."

"Thanks for inviting me," she said. "I've never done anything like this before."

"Of course," he said. "I'm just glad you said yes."

They sat in silence for a little bit, not knowing what to say. It was easier when Cleo was with them. It was nice to have an extra person to bounce conversation off of. But there was no way that they were going down to the main level to talk to Robert.

Don't think about it. Don't think about it.

All Hayes could think about was the picture.

All Lou could think about were her ghosts. The red baseball cap man had returned, setting a wet chill in the air. Her face fell. She had never seen him look so menacing before. His cap was pulled low over his eyes which had shadows beneath them as if he hadn't gotten any sleep.

But he is sleeping, Lou thought. *Sleeping eternally.*

The moment she blinked, he had disappeared.

Finally, Hayes could take it no longer.

"I really like you, Lou," he blurted. His eyes looked into hers, unwavering.

Something turned inside of Lou. It felt like she was Alice going *down, down, down* the rabbit hole. She was *falling, falling, falling,* desperately searching for the ground until she gave up and accepted the fact that she was going to fall forever.

He liked her.

Never, not in one million years did she think that she would be liked by someone like Hayes Dayholt. Kind, charming, effervescent Mr. Enterprise who always seemed to value others over himself.

Lou whispered, "I like you, too."

• • •

It was night at the Dayholt manor.

After dropping Lou off at ten, Hayes drove dreamily back home, feeling oddly light and ecstatic, the same way he did when he had too much caffeine while on cold medicine. He wanted Lou to stay later but there was no way that he was going to take *that* risk. After all, Myra knew his name.

He stretched out on the couch with his camera, reviewing more pictures. He had taken more that day, mostly for documentation but also to prove to himself that that picture of Lou and the red-cap man had been a fluke. Robert sat across from him on his phone in deep concentration.

He was probably playing candy crush.

Although there were no superfluous men with red caps in any of the shots he had taken, there was one which had an odd smear through the middle. It looked like mist. This didn't worry him. Water had probably sprayed on the lens.

Robert looked up from his phone, smirking.

"What are you so happy about?" Hayes snapped, still a little irritated about his brother's chlamydia comment.

"I know something you don't," he said in a singsong voice.

"Spill."

Robert cleared his throat.

Oh boy, Hayes thought.

"You know how I was saying that I recognized your beloved Miss Brightly?"

"Yes," Hayes said annoyedly. "Which was creepy, by the way."

Robert ignored him.

"So, I googled her, and you won't believe what I found."

"Robert!" Hayes yelled. "I've never seen you sink this low!"

After brief consideration, Hayes decided that he *had* in fact seen his brother sink this low. He shook his head. "You googled her?"

"*Shhh,*" Robert snapped his fingers twice, his signature symbol for *shut up.* "There's an entire documentary about her that was recorded about ten years ago."

Hayes' jaw dropped.

"You're serious?"

"Look," Robert impatiently pushed his screen into Hayes' face.

Hayes couldn't help but look. Robert had a YouTube video pulled up which had over ten million views. In the freeze frame was a picture of a young girl, maybe seven, with messy hair, freckles, and firefly hazel eyes.

It was, without a doubt, Lou.

"Holy shit," Hayes murmured.

"You think that's weird," Robert practically glowed, "take a look at this." He scrolled down to the title.

Hayes stared at it, letting the words sink in.

The Girl Who Walks with Shadows.

"What the Hell does that mean?" Hayes asked nervously, sinking his teeth into the side of his cheek.

Robert grunted. "It's pretty obvious, isn't it? It means ghosts, Hayes."

8

THE WARNING

Lou ran her fingers up and down Sunny's nose while her loyal pup snuggled closer into her chest. Lou lay between the cool sheets of her bed, thinking about Hayes. Her room was dark, but her mind was filled with the colorful memories of the afternoon on the yacht. *I like you. I like you, too.* The three little words meant so much to her. Her heart ballooned with every beat. Was this love? Or was she starved for the attention of someone who saw her as just plain Lou.

The clash between these thoughts swirled in her head until Sunny pulled her back to reality.

The tell-tale signs of a visitor. Sunny lifted her head. Her ears twitched, and she sniffed the air.

"What's wrong?" Lou asked, even though she knew all too well.

A spirit had arrived.

But something about this time was different. Usually Lou felt a slight chill and the ghost materialized within seconds. Now it was as if two forces were fighting for the front. Why they couldn't appear together, Lou didn't know. But they obviously were desperate to show themselves.

The air was hot with tension. She smelled caramel and cat hair and then something even more pungent. Was it sulfur?

Sunny began to growl, a trait very unusual for her.

A chill raced down Lou's spine and her hairs stood on end.

She gasped when her curtains started waving about, reaching towards her bed like long, hungry fingers. Her lamp on the bedside table light flicked on. Then off. Then on. Then off again.

Lou had never been afraid of her ghosts. They never gave her a reason to be afraid, but tonight the air felt dangerous, closing in on her with impending destruction. Her heart was gonna beat out of her chest. For a fleeting moment, she considered running. She knew there would be no sense in trying to take it on in a fight, but she had to get away. It was her versus them.

Her closet door opened.

Her stomach dropped.

The gap in the door grew larger. And larger. And larger, until…

Out stepped the old woman.

Sunny wagged.

Lou relaxed instantly, releasing all the air she had been holding with one giant exhale. her body fell back onto the bed in a giant heap, and she had to tilt her head up to look at the spirt.

The usually smiley woman looked grim.

"Hayes," she whispered.

Lou inhaled sharply. She had never heard the woman speak before.

"What?"

"Hayes," she repeated, her voice thin and croaky.

Lou tensed. Her fingers clutched at the sheets and the sense of impending doom from moments earlier returned.

"What about him?" she asked.

The old woman was already starting to fade, the outline of her body becoming increasingly fainter. She began slowly walking backward into the closet from where she came.

"What about him?" Lou urgently lunged forward as if to chase the visitor until she got her answer.

The grey woman had dissolved completely, but one last whisper floated through the air.

"Not him. The other one."

9

THE MAN IN THE DOORWAY

"When do you see them most?" A man behind the camera asked.

"They come whenever they want to." Seven-year-old Lou sat on a grey sofa, the camera zooming in on her small face. "A girl my age comes in the morning," she said. "She tells me *good morning*." She squirmed in her seat as little kids often do when they've been sitting in one place for too long.

"What else do you see?" The man behind the camera said.

"A man with a yellow coat. He carries a long pole with a hook on the end. A—a…"

"Fishing pole?" The man suggested.

"Yeah. A fishing pole," she said, but when she said it came out like *fwishing pole*. "And there's an old lady," she smiled, "she smells like candy."

The man chuckled, "Do you ever get scared?"

Lou blinked, "No. Real people scare me more."

The blue light of his laptop glowed onto Hayes' face, reflecting off of his prescription glasses that he begrudgingly wore at night. It was one in the morning. He couldn't sleep, so he sat on his bed with his computer propped up on his legs. His hair mused with the tossing and turning he had attempted a few hours prior, but he just couldn't get this new information out of his head. Hayes had spent the past two hours with his eyes locked on the documentary, *The Girl Who Walks with Shadows*.

He didn't know how he felt about all of this. Was it real? His mind kept circling back to the man with the red cap in the photograph. And then there was the one with a strange blur across it. *Could those be ghosts? They couldn't be.* How would this affect his relationship with Lou? He groaned. Now it was going to be weird. How could he look her in the eye and *not* tell her he knew?

The realization that she might not want to be with him now struck him fiercely. He was boring. Unspecial. Mundane. Wealth aside, there was nothing remarkable about him. Unlike Lou, no light emanated around him like a golden halo of extraordinary brightness.

Before his thoughts could spiral further, the documentary grabbed his attention once more.

The footage cut to a man who looked very reporter-esque with his navy-blue suit and microphone.

"This little girl has opened a broad gateway of opportunities for the better understanding of poltergeists. We can say with confidence that ghosts, without a doubt, are real. Spirits walk among us. We now hope to answer the questions, 'Exactly how many wandering souls are there?' 'What does this say about the afterlife?' and 'What does this mean for the future?'"

The screen faded, and the credits rolled. One of the first names to appear was *David Brightly.* Across from it read *paranormal specialist.* Hayes had always wondered what had happened to Lou's father, but he didn't want to pry. She never pried about his own father, so why should he pry about hers?

The rising sensation of guilt that comes when one falls too deeply into someone else's business tightened in his chest. Hayes closed his laptop. He shouldn't have watched the documentary. He should have told Robert to shove it. He should have pretended this never happened and he and Lou would date blissfully unaware of—

The door to his room opened, and the silhouette of a tall figure stood in the doorway. Hayes squinted.

"Dad?"

"Good morning." Miles replied coldly.

"You're back early," Hayes said, sitting up and turning on the light. Once his eyes had adjusted, he could see his father in full form: stony expression, thin hair, and a squared-off suit that made him look all the more terrifying.

"No need to state the obvious, son," He pulled out Hayes' chair from his desk and sat down. "We need to talk."

This couldn't be good. Whenever Hayes' dad wanted to *talk* it meant that he had gotten into a spot of trouble with his work. Hayes never fully understood what his father did for a living, nor did he care to ask, but occasionally his dad would give him certain *tasks* to complete.

"If someone, *anyone,* asks you where I've been the past two weeks, say I have been in Chicago."

Hayes frowned.

"But you just got back from Bali."

Miles pointed his index finger at his son, a signal that meant that he should be quiet.

"What do I always say to you, son?"

Hayes groaned. He hated being *son*. "Ask no questions. Need to know basis *only*."

"Right," his father asserted before continuing, "and this doesn't concern you any further than to tell a few white lies." As if it hadn't been clear enough already, he lowered his chin and stared into Hayes' eyes. "I have *not* been in Bali."

"Uh-huh," Hayes said flatly, disinterested. "You've been in Chicago."

"I'm glad we've gotten that established," Miles stood up and smoothed out his trousers. "Good-night."

"Night."

The moment after his father closed his door, Hayes reopened his laptop and entered *Bali* into the search engine. He dragged the cursor across the screen and hit the news icon. Apparently, it had been busy in Bali, for several articles had been posted in the last few hours. They all talked about one thing.

The murder of Clyde Grivins.

A lump formed in his throat. His father could be domineering, but he wasn't a murderer. This had to be a ridiculous coincidence.

Besides, if Hayes had been traveling in Bali and a murder had occurred, he would have been quick to deny that he had been anywhere near the island too, especially if he had as much fame and public recognition as his father.

The press could be merciless, and his father just didn't want to be associated with bad news, that's all. At least that's what he told himself. Hayes had enough to worry about already with Lou and the whole ghost business, so he wouldn't trouble himself further worrying about his dad. Miles had survived much worse.

For the final time that night, Hayes closed his laptop. He switched off the lights.

10

CLEO THE WWE FIGHTING CHAMPION

Ever since the night before, nothing had been quite right. Myra's healing crystals were disappearing and then reappearing in bizarre locations such as the ice tray, behind the tv, or in Lou's shoes. Windows and doors would open and close at random. Glasses of water would tip and spill seemingly without any help from an outside source.

"What's going on?" Myra asked that afternoon. She had just found her yoga mat draped from the ceiling fan and had had enough.

"I don't know," Lou didn't look at her mother as she carefully flipped an armchair back onto its legs.

Her mother was not convinced. "You must know *something*!"

Oh, she knew something alright. Lou had never experienced anything like she had on that night. There had never been such disturbance upon the arrival of an apparition before. Lou had a sinking feeling in her chest that there was a dark force at play. She had yet to see the old woman since the strange occurrence, and Lou had about a million questions for her.

Not him. The other one.

What did that mean? Was she referring to Cleo? And if so, what about Cleo? Was he in danger? Or was she warning her? Maybe they were the same.

Myra shook her head, "I'm going to go burn some sage or something. In the meantime, you think about if you have even an inkling of an idea about what's going on." Her mother left her with one last patronizing stare.

55

Lou rubbed her eyes with the heels of her hands. Maybe this was just a phase that would soon pass. Maybe if she distracted herself, it would go away? It didn't seem likely, but she didn't have any other ideas.

Lou had been waiting for Hayes to text her first since their date, but she caved and sent him a message saying, "I had fun, thanks for everything." She even decided to be risky and added a red heart emoji. Once that was settled, she pulled out her paper and charcoal. It had been a long time since she had drawn anything, and she got immense satisfaction from smearing the charcoal across the smooth paper with her thumb.

Hours passed.

She still hadn't heard back from Hayes.

This was very unusual for Mr. Enterprise, who normally responded within minutes. She frowned as she reviewed the text she had sent. She couldn't see anything wrong with it. *Maybe he's asleep,* she thought, but then she looked at the time to find that it was four in afternoon, so she pegged this theory as unlikely.

What was he up to?

Finally, she could take it no longer. She texted Cleo, "Have you heard from Hayes today?"

A few minutes later, he responded, "Yeah, why?"

Her stomach dropped. Her mind rushed back to Robert, looking at her inquisitively. *You look familiar. I've seen you somewhere before.*

The documentary. Robert must have shown Hayes the documentary.

Don't be ridiculous, she told herself. And yet, she still found herself panicking.

Maybe boys *were* scoundrels. But…she hadn't expected this one to be.

Lou's fingers flew across the cracked screen as she responded, "Can you come over?"

• • •

When Cleo arrived, he looked concerned.

"You okay?" His honey eyes searched her for an answer.

Lou bit her lip, trying to figure out how to get across what she was trying to say without bringing up the documentary. She fell into her silly habit of adjusting her bangs.

"I just...haven't heard from Hayes," she gulped, "and I think he might have found something out about me." Immediately, she regretted her words.

Ugh. Now he'll know, too, she thought.

Cleo sank back in his heels thoughtfully. His brows furrowed, and he looked at his feet as if he was considering if he should say something or not.

The tension was killing her.

His lips parted. "I know about the documentary."

Lou's heart seemed to stop beating. Her mind hummed as she tried to process this newfound information. *Cleo knew?*

"H-how long?" she demanded.

"For a while," he said casually, as if they were talking about vegetable gardens.

"Do you think Hayes—" she couldn't bring herself to ask the rest of the question.

"I know Hayes," he said sternly, "he wouldn't reject someone just because of a silly glimpse of their past."

But his face didn't look like he was so sure.

Lou dropped her hands to her sides.

Cleo's eyes flicked to her desk. He fingered one of her sketches of Sunny, a graphite mess of a job. But he held it gingerly, as if it were a priceless piece of art. He laid it back on her desk.

"Look," he said, "Hayes has always been tied down by his family. He's his father's puppet." He sighed, looking up at the ceiling. "I don't think he means to be an asshole, but sometimes he just is. It's in his genetic engineering."

"*Oh,*" Lou whispered as she sunk down onto her bed. Cleo was showing her a side of Hayes she had never seen before. It hurt.

"I'm going to go talk to him," he said, offering a supportive smile. He laughed, "The idiot's probably just gotten himself locked in his own bathroom."

Lou laughed, too, but it didn't make her feel any less terrible.

"Thanks," she smiled at him sweetly.

Cleo's boyish eyes crinkled at the corners.

"Anything for you."

• • •

Hayes ducked as the second punch came rocketing towards his nose. For a boy with scrawny arms who looked unathletic, Cleo could surely throw a fist directly on target.

Five minutes earlier, Cleo had texted him to meet him outside his house at the white gates. Cleo exited his car and without much announcement began rapidly attacking Hayes, swatting at his chest and swinging punches.

"What the hell?" Hayes shielded his face.

"Don't you dare hurt her!" Cleo yelled.

"Hurt who? You're hurting *me!*"

"Lou! Who else, dumbass?" Cleo grabbed Hayes who gripped him back and the boys wrestled to the ground, kicking and writhing on the pavement.

Hayes gritted his teeth, "I would never hurt her!"

"Then tell me you don't know about the documentary. Tell me you don't know!" Cleo managed to smack him across the cheek.

"Agh! Yes, I know, alright!"

Cleo stopped assaulting and Hayes pushed him off. The boys laid side by side on the hot cement. The blue sky stared down at them, and they watched the trees blow patterns across the sun.

"Not bad, Allegretti. I'm impressed."

"Shut up," Cleo breathed.

Hayes ignored him.

"Is that really what this is about? You think I'd brush her off because of *that?*"

"You've been ignoring her."

Hayes sighed. "Just been thinking about the next right thing to do." He lowered his voice, "I think I caught a ghost in one of the pictures I took of her."

Cleo's eyes widened and propped himself up on one elbow. "What?"

Hayes nodded. "I want to help her. I have so many questions. But I also don't want things to change," he said.

The sound of a car built up behind them.

The boys jumped to their feet, brushed off their clothes, and tried to appear as nonchalant as possible as they stood in the middle of the driveway.

A red Ferrari slowed, and the driver's seat window rolled down, revealing Miles Dayholt in all his grandiosity.

"Hello, boys," he tipped his glasses down to look them both in the eyes, disapprovingly.

"Hi," they said at once.

"What are you up to?"

Cleo and Hayes looked at each other and exchanged some silent communication.

What do we say?

I don't know! You think of something.

"Going for a walk," Hayes said.

Miles frowned. "Oh."

"See ya," Hayes said, ushering Cleo forward.

"Bye boys," Miles shook his head as he rolled up his window and drove through the gateway.

Cleo snickered, "Going for a walk? What, are we on our honeymoon?"

"You'd be lucky to even marry me. And I didn't see you coming up with any genius ideas."

"I think your dad is on to us," Cleo replied, ignoring Hayes' comment. His gaze trailing behind the red Ferrari.

"That's the other thing," Hayes looked fearfully at Cleo.

"What?"

"My dad is being weird. Weirder than usual," Hayes said simply.

"Weird how?" Cleo cocked his head.

"Well. I think he may have killed someone."

11

A BAD MAN MEDDLES

M any parents wonder why their kids are so lazy. Or obnoxious. Or thick-headed. But Miles Dayholt always wondered how his son had turned out so weird.

But wasn't being suspicious warranted?

Miles stormed into the mansion and set out to do what he would've never let his parents do when he was his son's age. He was going to search Hayes' room.

Hayes had always been relatively tidy, and the only sign of mess was to be found on his desk, where he kept a plethora of books, pictures, and... his *laptop*.

The laptop was barely distinguishable as a laptop amongst the mess, for Hayes had covered it top to bottom with various stickers. Miles lifted the screen and a password prompt popped up. Without missing a beat, he typed in his sons' birthday.

Vanity ran in the family.

The first thing that flashed across the screen was a headline about the murder in Bali.

Ah, just as Miles had expected. He had been preparing for this.

He closed the web browser and looked at the next icon that was open.

Photos.

He scrolled through the album mindlessly, amusing himself with his son's blissful ignorance of how the world worked. Nothing was this colorful.

He began to pay closer attention when he noticed a recurrence in the photos: a girl. There was a girl and a dog. The girl eating a burrito. The girl at the drive-in theatre.

Miles' hand froze on the keypad, and he pulled up an image of the girl standing in front of a crest, smiling. He recognized the hiking trail that he had bought a few summers back. It was seemingly normal, but something in the background caught his eye.

A man in a red baseball cap.

Miles slammed the laptop shut and backed away from the desk, horrified. How was this possible? He carefully lifted the screen again just to be sure that his eyes weren't deceiving him, but sure enough, Clyde Grivins was staring back at him.

A lump tightened in his throat, and he tried not to panic. After a minute of short, sharp breathing, Miles knew what he had to do. He needed to find out who this girl was. He wanted to know where she lived. He wanted to know what she had seen.

He wanted to know everything.

12

MEDIUM AT LARGE

Apologies were never Hayes' strength. What would he say to her? Something told him "I'm sorry for ignoring you because I watched a documentary about how you see ghosts" wasn't going to cut it.

But at least he had a plan.

Well, half of one.

He pulled up to the little yellow house with significantly less gusto on the overcast Monday morning. Cleo sat beside him. He had chosen to bring him along because history suggested that Cleo was proficient in damage control.

Well, unless you counted the previous day, when Cleo had attacked him.

Lou looked particularly beautiful today, a detail that made it much more intimidating for Hayes. She stepped out onto the front porch delicately, the length of her legs accentuated by her black jean shorts. Her eyes glowed in the greyness of the day.

"Hello," she said.

Sunny sat at her side, looking at the boys curiously.

Hayes was to the point: "I'm sorry," he said, sliding his hands in his pockets.

Cleo, who had been watching him carefully, tilted his head as if to say *and?*

"I was an asshole."

Cleo nodded, satisfied.

Lou stepped down from the porch and took her time striding over to Hayes, Sunny at her heel. She stopped inches away and looked up at him.

"Thanks for coming back," she smiled.

"I never left," he said.

There was a long moment where it felt like there was nothing but the two of them as they looked into one another's eyes.

Cleo rocked on his heels.

"Alright Ross and Rachel, let's go."

"Where are we going?" Lou asked, breaking from her trance.

"To the medium," Hayes said.

• • •

There was a lot of explaining to be done on the drive to the medium's house, which was over three hours away on the outskirts of Orange County.

"So, you're telling me that you think your dad killed someone?" Lou raised her brows.

"Seems to be that way. He doesn't want anyone to know that he had been in Bali."

"Uh oh," Lou said. "That could be a problem."

Hayes jammed on the breaks and the tires squealed on the road. "What do you mean?"

"Hayes!" Cleo yelled. "Focus on driving, please!"

If Hayes' driving had been skeptical before, it was definitely bad enough to put anyone on edge when he was distracted.

Lou continued, "It was published in the local paper weeks ago—in the article about his donation. It said that he was in Bali. I know because my mom told me. She's into all of that spiritual well-being stuff, and she's obsessed with your dad because she thinks he has problems," she said matter-of-factly.

"Shit," Hayes muttered.

It was bad enough that his father had been on the island, but it was going to be even more suspicious if he was caught lying about it. Hayes walked a fine line between questioning his father...and wanting to protect him.

"I need to find out more," he said, mostly to himself. "In the meantime, let's figure out your ghosts. I saw on yelp that this medium is supposed to be something of a legend."

Lou swallowed. She had yet to relay the events of the haunting. *Not him. The other one.* Maybe she better keep that to herself for now. She didn't want to cause any alarm. Although wasn't keeping secrets the thing that had pushed Hayes away in the first place?

Lou couldn't stop herself from looking back at Cleo, who was absentmindedly peering at a seagull that flew overhead. Was he *the other one?*

She hoped Hayes was right about this medium.

• • •

The medium's house was secluded on the peak of a grassy hill. At first Lou thought that the ground was entirely dirt, but it had just browned in the sun.

"This looks homey, in a haunted house kind of way," Cleo said.

The house, or, more appropriately, the shack, had once been blue, but the paint had chipped and weathered away. It had a new-looking tin roof which looked horrendously out of place sitting on top of the abomination. A small, lopsided sign hung from one chain over the doorway. *Leona Finch. Medium.* Beneath that hung a smaller sign which said *Cash only.*

"Do we go in?" Hayes asked.

The three of them stood on the wonky wooden porch, which didn't look like it should've been able to support the three of them.

"I don't know," Cleo said. "You got cash?"

Lou was skeptical, but eager for answers.

"Let's go," she said, lifting the latch on the door, which creaked like something from a horror movie.

If the outside had been creepy, the inside was creepier. Cobwebs strung across the exposed beams of the ceiling, and years of dust had collected on the windows, blocking out most of the sunlight. There was minimal furniture, namely a round table that sat in the middle of the room. In the middle, a candle was lit, which reflected light off of two large, round, misty eyes.

The unseeing eyes blinked, and the three of them shuddered.

No wonder it's so dark, Lou thought. *She doesn't need any light to see.*

They watched her remain motionless, and Cleo whispered to Hayes, "Maybe she's dead."

"Don't be ridiculous," he said. "I saw her blink."

They jumped when a shriveled hand reached across the table and pointed at Lou's chest.

"The spirits like you," the woman said.

• • •

Myra wondered where Lou had gone with the boys, for it had been hours since they left. Truth be told, she was actually a little glad about it because it meant that she got a break from what she called "all the paranormal shit."

After doing a ten minute-meditation, she stretched and strolled out to the end of the driveway to collect the mail. Snail mail, in her opinion, was useless and wasted too many trees. But bills had to be paid one way or another, and it would never happen if she let them sit in the mailbox.

She shuffled through a few envelopes, one from a wildlife reserve asking for a donation, a bill, and a nice creamy envelope with an old-fashioned wax seal on the front. Myra frowned. She thought that they only used wax seals in the 1500s and in *Harry Potter.* She flipped it over and gaped at the return address.

It was from Miles Dayholt.

Of course he liked snail mail. And wax seals.

Her hands quivered slightly as she tore open the envelope. She could imagine what this was going to be about. *Please tell your daughter to stop hanging out with my son. It's bad for our public image.* Maybe he had even filed a lawsuit. She didn't want to imagine what kind of powerhouse lawyers Miles Dayholt had at his right hand.

But it wasn't a letter.

It was an *invitation.*

We would be so pleased if you and your daughter Lou would join us for dinner on the 14th of July. We will send a car for you at 6pm.

Regards,

Miles Dayholt.

She scoffed.

"No need to ask if we accept," she muttered to an empty street.

But it was Miles Dayholt. She had no say.

13

AURAS AND THE COLOR RED

The medium had the three of them sit around the table, the light of the candle glowing on their faces.

"You have a very strong aura, my girl," she said to Lou. After a moment of silence, she added, "You do know what an aura is, don't you children?"

Cleo and Hayes wiggled in their seats, visibly annoyed at being called *children*.

Lou rolled her eyes.

"Um...isn't it like energy that has a distinct color depending on the person?" Cleo offered.

The woman tilted her head back and cackled.

"You are adorable," she croaked, "This isn't Buzzfeed, my boy." She continued to roar with laughter.

Cleo chuckled, too, mostly because he was uncomfortable.

Hayes straightened into full Mr. Enterprise form. "If we could please, er, ma'am— "

"Call me Leona."

"Right, uh, Leona, if we could get back to business, that would be excellent."

"Why the rush, my dear?"

She honed in on him, leaning fervently across the table, and Hayes sat back as far as he could in his chair without tipping over.

Lou rescued him.

"I see ghosts," she said calmly.

Without turning her head, the woman said, "I know. They are telling me right now."

Out of the corner of her eye, Lou saw Cleo scanning the room.

"How many can you see now, darling?" Leona asked.

Lou looked around. "I can't see anything. I don't really have control over when I can see them," she said.

"Ah. No one does."

"Then why did you ask?"

"Just curious," Leona said, and she trailed off, humming quietly to herself and sinking into the back of her chair.

Hayes raised his brows at Cleo and Lou as if to ask, *Was that it?*

But then the woman jolted upright, making the three of them jump.

"As I was saying before I was interrupted," she said to Lou, "you have a powerful aura. The energy that you emote encloses you in a protective bubble, if you will," she nodded towards Cleo. "That is an aura, my boy."

Cleo nodded slowly, still bewildered.

She turned back to Lou. "Part of the reason why the souls are attracted to you is because they feed off of your aura to become stronger."

"I have been seeing more ghosts than usual," Lou said. "What does that mean?"

"Well, your aura must have become increasingly forceful as of late. What has changed?"

"Well..." Lou's gaze shifted to Cleo and Hayes.

"Ah, I understand," the woman said. "I sense that these boys have given you a greater wholeness. Friendship can do that. But be wary. Oftentimes people find ways to weaken their aura in order to minimize the visits from the spirits."

"What do you mean?" Lou asked.

"Some drink. Others turn to drugs. And some just stop enjoying life's greatest pleasures. An old book. A summer's breeze. Cold hands on a warm cup of coffee. Some even give up eating in order to wither away into spirits themselves."

Lou and Cleo locked eyes. Her cheeks burned.

"Okay," she laughed uneasily, "I'll keep that in mind."

"Of course you will, my dear," Leona said.

And then her face darkened.

"What's that?" Leona said, although it was clear that the question wasn't directed at any of the three of them. She tilted her head to one side and pursed her lips. "Oh, mercy."

"What?" The three asked at once.

Leona lifted a wrinkled, shaking finger at Lou. Although the woman was blind, Lou felt as if the woman could see more of her than anyone else ever could.

"Do not underestimate spirits," she said, and the flame on the candle puffed, sending sparks shooting across the room. The air chilled.

Lou shivered. "What do you mean?"

The woman smiled, "You know what I mean." She leaned in close and whispered in her ear, "It's best not to go against their wishes."

Lou inhaled sharply, and one thought crossed her mind.

Not him. The other one.

"But what if I don't understand," she whispered back.

"You'll understand soon enough," she said, her head turning to the two boys who were nervously biting their lips.

The room resumed normality.

"That will be all, thank you," she folded her hands.

"Wait," Lou said, slamming her hand down on the table.

"I would prefer if you wouldn't hit my table, dear, it was Amish-made."

"I'm sorry," she said quickly and removed her hands from the table-top as if it burned her. "Are there ever any...bad spirits?"

"Lou—" Hayes grabbed her arm.

"No," she said. "I want to know." She stared at the woman, whose head was tilted up to the ceiling. She seemed to be thinking.

The question hung in the air for an excruciatingly long minute.

Finally, the woman said, "Bad? No. Troubled? Yes. And they can do terrible things."

Lou's heart pounded in her chest. She thought that she had

already known the answer to this question, but hearing it from a medium affected her more than she thought it would.

She gulped, "Thank you for your time."

Cleo and Hayes both fumbled for their wallets, but the woman stopped them, saying, "Don't you young-ins worry about it. I do these sessions for free."

"But then why do you have the sign?"

"I think it's funny," she said.

They looked at each other and shrugged.

The woman cackled once more, "You try reading paper money when you're blind, kiddos, and you'll understand."

Hayes just *hmm'ed* and placed a few bills beneath an empty water glass anyways.

"Thanks again," Cleo said.

"Oh, no need to thank me, darlings," she sighed. "You have enough to worry about already."

• • •

Rather than reassuring him, the visit with the medium had made Hayes feel even more in the dark than before. He thought back to the cobwebbed room when the old woman leaned in close and whispered in Lou's ear. He had watched Lou's face fall. For the first time, Hayes had seen her look scared.

Never underestimate spirits.

It felt like something much bigger than him was ahead.

He paced in his bedroom, listening to the rain clatter against the window. The cloudy day had finally turned into a stormy one. He felt restless as he walked back and forth, back and forth across the room. He wanted answers, but the pile of questions only seemed to grow. On top of all the ghost business, he wanted to know the truth about his father. What had he been up to in Bali?

Suddenly, he stopped.

Hayes had an idea, but he wasn't sure if he had the gumption to do it.

He cracked his bedroom door open and peeked down the hall-way. His father's door was closed. That could mean one of two things. Either his father was brooding and wanted to be alone, or he had left the house.

Hayes decided to try his luck.

He carefully turned the door handle, flinching at the slightest creak.

But his father wasn't there.

Hayes let out a huge breath of air he had been holding and scanned the room. Even the act of looking felt criminal. Miles Dayholt had a strict "Don't go into my room" policy.

A pretty vague rule.

The room looked like it belonged to a physicist, an artist, or an author. It was the abode of a man who was obsessed. The king-sized bed was unmade, and random articles of clothing were sprawled along the bedspread. A wrinkled shirt here. A sock there. The wastebasket in the corner was overflowing with crumpled up papers.

But what Hayes really wanted was sitting at the foot of the bed.

His father's luggage.

The sound of him unhooking the latch was deafening.

"Shh!" he scolded the worn suitcase.

The second Hayes lifted the lid, he gasped and backed up until he hit the wall behind him. His hands began to sweat. His heart skipped.

He couldn't believe his eyes.

The contents of the case had mostly been removed, although there were a few miscellaneous objects. A watch. A pair of glasses. A few post it notes with scrawled handwriting, some underwear. . .

And a red baseball cap.

14

A GIFT FROM THE RAIN

When Myra asked where Lou had been all day, she said with the utmost composure, "Parasailing."

"Parasailing?" Her mother had her hands on her hips, one eyebrow arched high above the other.

Lou knew that she shouldn't lie to her mother, especially after what happened the last time. But she knew that if she told her mother about the medium, the amount of follow up questions would be endless.

Lou shrugged.

Myra squinted.

"I thought you were mad at Hayes," she said.

"Not mad" Lou corrected, "agitated."

"What's the difference?"

"The longevity," she said.

Myra shook her head.

"Well I'm glad you're not *agitated* anymore because I just received an invitation from Mr. Dayholt. We're having dinner at his house on the fourteenth."

"What?"

Lou's heart dropped into her stomach. She was remembering the conversation she had had with Hayes and Cleo that morning on the way to the medium's house. The one where he suspected Miles had killed someone.

It started to rain. This was highly unusual for California in July, the cherry on top of Lou's strange day.

"Weird, isn't it?" her mother said.

"What, the rain?"

"No, dinner!" she said, whacking Lou's arm playfully. Then she lowered her voice, "How serious is your relationship with Hayes? If they ask me for my permission for you to marry him, I swear— "

"*Mother!*" Lou shouted, turning red.

"Just checking," she smiled and held up her hands defensively.

There was a knock at the door, and Sunny perked her ears.

"I'll get it," Lou said, starting for the front door. Sunny trotted along at her heels, ready to attack if need be. Lou swung the door open.

Cleo stood on the front porch, soaking wet. His jacket was rain-spattered, and his brown curls stuck to his face.

"God Cleo, you must be freezing!" Lou held the door open a but wider. "Do you want to come in?"

He shook his head, sending droplets of rain flying in every direction.

"No. I just forgot something."

Lou noticed that he was holding something behind his back, and she leaned to try to get a better look. He smiled and produced two small packages wrapped in yellow, polka-dotted wrapping paper.

"You know my birthday isn't until March, right?" she asked.

"I know," he handed the presents to her, the wrapping only slightly damp.

Lou tore at the paper. *Please don't be something ridiculously expensive,* she thought.

She uncovered a sketchbook and a nice packet of professional-grade oil pastels.

"I figured you might like them," he explained, "I saw the art on your desk, and I thought you could make something really beautiful with these."

Lou grinned, unable to hide her pleasure.

"Thank you," she said, throwing her arms around his shoulders.

He caught her a tad shakily and eased into the hug.

A million thoughts raced through Lou's mind as she hugged

Cleo. Namely, she thought of Hayes, and what he would think about her standing there in the rain, hugging his best friend.

She let go.

"Thank you," she said again.

Cleo smiled, wide and boyish, "You're always welcome, Lou."

With that, he ran back to his car, not bothering to try to shield himself from the rain.

Lou turned the pastels over in her hands. Was this gift supposed to mean something? If so, what? Sunny managed to push the door open wide enough so she could slip through, and she sat next to Lou, pressing her wet nose to Lou's palm.

Not him. The other one.

What did it mean?

Lou sighed. Cleo had always been precious to her, but she knew where her heart truly lay...with Hayes Dayholt.

From inside the house, there came a shrill scream.

15

SOME PROFANITY

Lou bolted into the house just before her mother screamed for the second time, after which she yelled in a high pitch voice at the top of her lungs, "What the fuck?"

"Mom!" she found her mother in the kitchen backed against the counter, clutching the sides of the kitchen sink like they were her savior. "Are you ok?"

Sunny skipped over to Myra and began licking her legs affectionately.

Her mother's hair looked wilder than usual, her curls seeming to stand on end. She stared into the living room, but Lou couldn't see anything there.

"Mom?" Lou repeated.

Myra gasped, "I just—I just. . ."

"You just what?"

"I just saw a ghost!"

Lou's heart skipped a beat.

"You *what?*"

"Saw a ghost, dammit! Right there," she pointed to the living room. "He-he was older. Fifties maybe."

"Go on," Lou urged. "What was he wearing?"

"A red baseball cap!"

"Then what happened?"

"Nothing! He just vanished!" Myra shook her head like she was trying to erase the memory.

"It's okay," Lou said, unconvincingly. "I'll figure out what's going on."

"Lou," her mother grabbed her arm, "Whatever is happening, it feels dangerous. I'm sure I'll never understand ghosts in the same way you do, but you need to be careful, you hear me?"

"I hear you, mom."

She held up one quivering finger, "If you can't sort this out, I might have to call your father."

It was Lou's turn to say, "Fuck."

• • •

Miles Dayholt was not in a good mood. He returned home to find that his suitcase was a tad slighter to the right than he had left it. He may have been messy, but it was an organized mess.

Someone had been in his room.

"Hayes?" he called.

"Yeah?" came a distant voice from down the hall.

Miles stomped to his son's bedroom and knocked on the door as he opened it.

Hayes was on his bed flipping through a book.

Miles wasn't buying it. Hayes hardly ever read.

"Son?" he asked as genially as possible, "Did you go into my room?"

"Nope," Hayes said without missing a beat.

"Oh, ok. That's all," Miles didn't buy that either. But that wasn't all. "Oh, and son?"

Hayes snapped the book shut and looked up.

"Yes, father?"

"I invited Lou Brightly and her mother Myra over for dinner on Friday. Just thought you should know."

Hayes jumped to his feet, kicking about three throw blankets to the floor as he did so.

"H-how do you know about her?"

Miles cocked his head as if he were thinking, "Oh, you know. Myra and I have been friends for *years*."

"If you're trying to be funny, you're not," Hayes snapped.

"I mean no offense, son," he assured his son, holding his hands up apologetically. "I just have a striking suspicion that your little friend Lou is a real *cool ghoul*." He chuckled in a way that reminded Hayes of Dr. Frankenstein.

Hayes plastered on the fakest smile he could muster.

"See you later dad," he said, slinging the door closed.

Miles stared at the whiteness of the door in his face. He had always figured Robert was the more intelligent of his two sons, but Hayes was proving to be quite *something*.

Things were just beginning.

16

COFFEE WITH LEONA

Lou received a series of texts from Hayes late at night, a consistent habit of his.

"My dad invited you and your mom to dinner?!"

Followed by, "You knew about this?"

And then, "Can I call you?"

Before Lou could respond to any of the questions, her phone started to ring.

"Hayes— "

"You won't believe what has just happened," he said. There was a lot of rustling noise and Lou thought he might have been pacing.

"Well, I was just about to say the same thing. You first," she said.

"So, my dad is on to us. I don't know how he found out about you, but he knows."

"You sure you or Robert never mentioned my name to him, even by accident?"

"Are you kidding?" Hayes said, "Who talks to their parents any-more?"

Lou had to chuckle at that one. She would have replied that *she* still did, if it weren't for the sneaking around and lying about activities as of late.

"And that's only a small part," he said. "I looked through his luggage, and you won't believe what I found!"

Lou wrinkled her brow.

"What?"

"A *red baseball cap.*"

She made a noise in the back of her throat.

"Hayes, I'm sure multiple people in the world have a red baseball cap, and I don't see what that has to do with anything."

"Your ghost!" He said. "The picture!"

"You think your dad killed him?"

"Yes! Somehow, he found out that I had been in his room—maybe he has cameras or something—anyways, he confronted me, and he was *definitely* upset about it."

She sighed, "Hayes— "

Suddenly, Lou had an epiphany.

When had she first seen the man with the red cap?

On the hike with Cleo and Hayes.

He remembered the way he had looked at her, face stony and eyes sunken.

And just that afternoon, her mother had seen him. Her *mother*, who never saw a ghost before a day in her life.

There were too many coincidences.

"Holy shit," Lou breathed. She took a moment to compose herself before relaying the events of what transpired just a few hours ago.

When she was done, she let Hayes have a moment to think about it. She knew the rapid-fire pace of new information had to make anyone's head spin.

He pondered for a moment before asking, "What does this mean?"

"You tell me," she answered.

"Friday is sure going to be interesting," Hayes chuckled, but there was an undertone of anxiety in his voice. He had no idea what his father had in store.

"I know what I have to do," Lou said.

This startled Hayes.

"What?"

"Tomorrow I'm going back to the medium. And I'm going alone."

"Lou—"

She hung up before Hayes could talk her out of it.

• • •

Lou didn't think she would be returning to the medium so soon, if ever. The drive wasn't as fun in her mom's Honda. She missed the convertible. She missed the boys. But she needed to do this alone. Lou felt that Leona withheld some information in the last session. Was it because Cleo and Hayes had been there? Only one way to find out.

Her phone buzzed in the center console, but Lou disregarded it. Cleo and Hayes had been texting her all morning trying to talk her out of it, and she had been ignoring them religiously. She had seen ghosts her entire seventeen years of life. She would be fine. She just needed answers.

It was sunny that day, and the light reflected off of the old woman's fresh tin roof with blinding beams. Lou shaded her eyes as she walked up to the crooked front porch. Besides the sunshine, nothing had changed, and the door squeaked like an out of tune violin.

The woman sat at the round table, candlelight glowing in her misty eyes.

"You again?" she asked.

"Yes," Lou tried to make her voice sound as even as possible in lieu of letting the old woman know that she gave her the creeps.

"Coffee?" The woman asked, ungracefully getting on her feet.

Lou sprang into action.

"I'll get it," she said, striding over to the shiny new electric coffee pot which looked infinitely out of place in Leona's raggedy home.

"Thank you, dear," she said, settling back in her seat.

Lou found two mugs in a cupboard and poured the inky coffee.

"Didn't expect you to be a coffee person," she said bluntly from the kitchen, mesmerized as the sound and smell of her favorite beverage sank into the bottom of each cup. Focusing on it helped calm her nerves.

"What's wrong with coffee?"

"Nothing. I love coffee," Lou insisted, "It's just that I always thought psychics and what not drank tea."

Leona grumbled, "I'm a medium, darling, not a shrink. You watch too much bad television."

Lou snorted at the remark as she placed one of the mugs in front of the old woman and sat down opposite her.

"My mother always tells me that coffee throws off her spiritual balance."

The woman considered this.

"That may be true. But it's delicious," she sipped vivaciously and slammed her mug down on the table. "But you didn't come here to talk about coffee, did you, dear?"

"I want answers."

The old woman smiled, seeming to reminisce on something. "Ah, don't we all. I notice you didn't bring your friends this time."

Lou faltered.

"Well, I thought that maybe— "

"You want to know more than what they can handle?"

"...Yes," she said reluctantly.

Leona nodded, "Good. Ask away, then."

She cleared her throat. "First," Lou began, "I want to know who you were talking to yesterday during the session. I could tell it was some sort of spirit, but who?"

"Aha!" The woman lit up. "We'll get to that all in good time. Ask a different question."

"Well...okay...?" Lou said, caught off guard. "Yesterday my mom saw one of the ghosts I've been seeing more frequently in the living room. But...she's never seen ghosts before!"

"Love," the woman whispered.

Lou choked on the coffee, which tasted terrible.

"What?" she coughed out, lightly rubbed at the front of her throat to soothe the ache.

"Love," she repeated. "Love makes the aura stronger. When the aura is at its strongest, ghosts can use the energy to be seen by people who normally cannot see. In extreme cases, they can even materialize."

Lou gulped.

"The question is, *who do you love?*" The way the woman said the last four words sent a chill down her spine.

"I don't know."

The woman smiled deviously, "Oh but you do. And it's not *the other one.*"

Lou jolted forward and grabbed the other woman's hands tightly.

"How do you know about that?"

Leona's unseeing eyes never left Lou's as she answered, "I was just getting to that. The spirit I was talking to yesterday at our little meeting, was none other than Clyde Grivins."

"Clyde Grivins?" Lou furrowed her brow. The name meant nothing to her.

"He wears a red cap," Leona said absentmindedly.

Lou saw a flash in her mind and suddenly two puzzle pieces were fitted together. She tried to maintain her composure as Leona continued.

"Clyde happens to be a troubled soul," she said, leaning back into her chair. "Oh, so troubled."

Lou remembered the previous day and what the woman had said about troubled souls. *They can do terrible things.* Worse yet, this troubled soul happened to be stalking her.

"I don't understand. What does this have to do with Cleo and Hayes? Besides, it wasn't Clyde's ghost who warned me, it was an old woman."

"The old woman," Leona said slowly, "was warning you about Mr. Grivins, I'm afraid. If you choose your dear friend Hayes over—what's his name?"

"Cleo!" she nearly shouted over the adrenaline pumping through her veins.

"Right, right. If you choose Hayes over Cleo, something terrible is bound to happen."

"What? Why? What do they—" Lou's stomach twisted in a knot. Her eyes had started to water, but she blinked the tears back furiously. *Don't you dare cry,* she thought. Even though she knew that the old woman couldn't see her, she was determined to preserve a piece of her dignity. She wiped her palms on the sides of her shorts. "How? Why?"

"Revenge," Leona said blankly.

"I don't understand," Lou said, voice shaking. "Why would— "

"Because Clyde's murderer is none other than Miles Dayholt."

17

CONTACT

Lou agonized the entire trip home. She kept thinking, *why me? Why me!?* Why would Hayes have to pay the price for her love? And what about Cleo? Oh, Cleo. He was precious to her, but she could never love him fully enough if she was forced to part ways with Hayes.

"I love them both," she said to herself. "I can't do this to them."

She couldn't be selfish. Clyde Grivins wanted revenge, and Hayes was his target. Lou was the gateway. There was no way she was going to put his life in jeopardy. And if something *did* happen, Cleo would lose his best friend.

The tears which Lou had expected, but dreaded, seemed to pour out of her eyes, one after the other. They hit the seat of her mother's Honda with faint tapping noises.

It was time to say goodbye.

One little detail popped into her head: the dinner with Miles.

Dinner be damned, she thought. *There is no way I'm going.*

No matter how many times she told herself this, she knew deep down that she *had* to go. Lou didn't want to think about what would happen if she and her mother bowed out.

Miles Dayholt, she thought, *is a troubled soul.*

• • •

Lou was determined not to read the texts Cleo and Hayes were sending her, but the constant vibration of her phone was making it all the more difficult. Eventually she turned it off, wrapped it in a towel, and shoved it in a drawer. Just in case.

She hadn't told her mother about the medium's warning, but Myra noticed the difference in Lou's behavior immediately.

"Stop sulking around all the time," she said at the breakfast table one morning. "You look like Wednesday Addams."

When Lou didn't respond and poked around at her oatmeal, her mother sighed.

"Is it something about the boys?"

"Yep," she said shortly.

"Care to tell you mom about it? Or are we not doing that whole communication thing?"

Lou grumbled, "It's a *me* problem."

Myra closed her eyes as if she were meditating.

"Hold a healing crystal, or something," Myra said. "Try a juice cleanse. Take a yoga class." She grabbed her plate and tossed it in the sink. "I want my happy girl back."

As soon as her mother left the room, Lou let her spoon clatter in her bowl, defeated. She was back to square one.

Some ghosts.

And no friends.

Throughout the day, she found things that urged her to remember the friendship that *had been.* Cleo's oil pastels. The pot of blue and white geraniums that sat in her windowsill. Everywhere she looked Lou found something that reminded her of them. Even the old woman, who visited in the early afternoon, with her tight smile and eyes that said *I'm sorry* was now a symbol of defeat.

Sunny rested her head on Lou's knee and whined. Even her dog missed them.

"Come on," she said, putting her shoes on.

Out in the California sun, Lou's little rain cloud followed close behind. Sunny had perked up, stopping to sniff excitedly at a caterpillar here, a dandelion there. Lou adjusted her grip on Sunny's new leash. Even the way she walked her dog had changed.

She considered adjusting her usual route so she wouldn't have to pass Waterloo Drive, but Sunny was tugging so hard on her arm that she relented.

Just as long as I don't see any silver convertibles, I'll be fine, she thought.

Sunny stopped pulling and began to wag.

"Oh, you've *got* to be kidding me," Lou whispered.

Up ahead, a silver BMW convertible was parked at the curb.

"You can't avoid me forever."

Lou jumped and whirled around to find that Hayes had snuck up behind her. He looked extra Mr. Enterprise-y today with his designer sunglasses.

"Hello," Lou said, stuffing her free hand in her pocket.

He knelt down to pet Sunny's head.

"Okay so let's cut to the chase," he said, standing up abruptly. "Where have you been, Lou?"

Lou couldn't look him in the eyes.

"I can't do this, Hayes."

"Yeah? Well, try." He shifted his feet. "I miss you." The last three words sounded almost like a plea, but she knew someone of his status would never stoop low enough to beg. Or so she thought.

"Don't make this harder than it needs to be," she said.

"What the hell did that medium tell you?" His voice cracked and he grabbed her wrists tightly.

"Listen," Lou said, lowering her voice. "You know the man with the red cap?"

"Yeah?" His grip only grew tighter.

"His name is Clyde Davis. You were right, Hayes.. Your dad... he..." she couldn't even bring herself to say it.

Hayes backed up, throwing his hands up to his head.

"Holy shit, are you serious? H-he didn't. He's not a *murderer*." The last word barely escaped past his lips in a whisper.

"This spirit is dangerous, Hayes. The medium warned me that I need to stay away from you."

"What?" Hayes shook his head as if he hadn't heard the words right. "Why would you need to stay away from me?"

"Clyde wants revenge." Lou looked away so he couldn't see the tears that were beginning to form. "You're his target. Even right now I'm probably putting you in danger," she said, backing away.

Hayes kicked at a pebble.

"Bullshit."

"What?" she sniffled. "Hayes, I'm serious! The medium said—"

"I don't care what that crazy medium says. Why should I pay the price for something my dad did?" He reached her in three strides. This close together, she could feel the heat emanating off his body. She could see the faint freckles dotting different parts of his face. And she could smell his signature cologne, a smell so *him* that her head swam.

Trying to regain composure, she began again, "Clyde is dangerous, Hayes. If we stay together something is going to happen!" Her voice strained against her own throat, but he had to listen to her. She wasn't going to take any chances.

Hayes scoffed before his facial expression turned softer.

He brought one hand up to light smooth down her hair. When it reached the end it ran it along her cheek to rest on the side of her neck. She watched as his lips barely opened and he whispered, "I can't lose you."

Before Lou could do anything, both hands came up to cup her face and pulled her in for a desperate kiss.

Sunny, very satisfied with her work, wagged her tail.

• • •

I'm going to help you figure this out.

Hayes' words echoed in her head and the taste of his kiss lingered on her lips. Her heart fluttered as she walked home, every step a beat to a Beatle's song that was stuck in her head. Maybe the medium had been wrong. They had to be wrong sometimes, right? Like psychics.

Lou knew that this didn't make any sense. But she had just

kissed the boy she wasn't supposed to be around, and nothing bad had happened.

At least not yet.

There was still the dinner to get through, though.

Lou was humming when she got home, and Myra couldn't help but notice the drastic change in attitude.

"How was the walk?" her mother called from the kitchen where she was washing dishes.

"Good," Lou chirped.

"You've sure perked up," Myra threw a towel over her shoulder and suppressed a smile.

Lou was already walking out of the kitchen as she spoke, "Yeah," she said, pausing a long second for suspense. "I just had my first kiss." Before her mother said anything, she had walked right into her room and softly closed the door.

From the other room, Lou heard a dish clatter to the floor.

She chuckled at her mom's reaction to her admission and pulled out her phone from the towel in the drawer. Her right hand came up to fiddle with the soft petals of the blue geraniums while her left scrolled through the texts the boys had sent her over the past couple of days. She was sorry that she ever ignored them. If there was one thing Lou learned that summer, it was that it wasn't always better to do things alone.

"Lou!"

She dropped her phone down on the bed carelessly. Her mother was calling her from the kitchen. *It's about the kiss,* she thought. Cautiously, she slipped out of her room and paced quietly to the kitchen.

Immediately, she dismissed the idea of it having anything to do with the kiss.

Myra stood on edge in front of the fridge, eyes wide.

In front of her stood the little girl with the ruddy cheeks, who held out her hand.

"Mom— "

"Shh!" her mother hissed.

93

She reached back.
The little girl beamed.
"Lou," Myra gasped, "I can *feel* her!"

18

THE DINNER PARTY

"Remember, we're getting picked up at six!" Myra yelled over the whirring of the hair dryer that Lou was attacking her own head with.

Lou only turned the dryer off long enough to mutter, "Kill me now."

Even though she had vetoed cutting out Cleo and Hayes from her life, Lou was dreading to meet the man who may have killed someone. The same man who had mysteriously found out all about her—her name, her mother's name, where they lived. The man who always showed up in the news wearing sunglasses and an expression that Lou used to think was a smile, but now pegged as a sneer.

The problem was, Hayes came with a father.

After the incident with the little girl, Lou had been extraordinarily on edge.

"I just don't understand how it's possible!" her mother had said.

Lou didn't exactly take to the idea of explaining to her mother about *auras, materialization* and what not, so she had slipped out of the room. She relayed the events to Hayes and Cleo over the phone.

"Did the medium say this would happen?" Cleo asked.

"I was wrong to ever take Lou to the medium, Cleo, let's just assume it's all BS," Hayes grumbled.

"She didn't say it would happen," Lou interjected, "but she said it was possible."

"Thank you!" Cleo said.

"Look, I'm sure it'll all be fine," Hayes said. "The only thing we have to worry about now is keeping Lou safe. I'm not sure what my dad wants, but he must know about the connection between her and Clyde. I don't know how, but he does."

"Is there any way we can get out of the dinner?" Lou asked, already knowing the answer.

"When my dad wants something," Hayes said grimly, "he gets it."

"Lou, the...the car is here."

Oh no, she thought. She could only imagine what kind of car Miles Dayholt had sent for them. She inspected her outfit, which was a fitted cream dress. Once she deemed it *classy enough,* Lou brushed on some dark cherry lipstick and bustled out of the bathroom.

Myra was looking out of the front window, mouth gaping.

"How bad is it?" Lou asked.

"It's a *fucking Lamborghini!*"

• • •

The drive to the Dayholt mansion had been infinitely more fun with the boys—the wind whipping around the convertible as Queen blared on the radio. Not to mention the good company. The only company in the small, stuffy Lamborghini that smelled like leather and shoe polish was a chauffeur named *Chad,* who only spoke in gestures.

He held the door open and gestured: *get in.*

When her mother asked how long of a drive it would be, he gestured: *none of your business.*

When Lou asked how his day had been, he gestured: *don't talk to me.*

Finally, it happened.

They arrived.

Lou's stomach twisted and turned as they pulled up beneath the veranda. Myra had been marveling since the great white gates, an exclamation here, a profanity there. Now that Lou had a better understanding of who the owner of the great mansion was, it appeared ominous, almost sinister.

Lou brightened when she saw Hayes waiting for them beneath the veranda. He was wearing a perfectly tailored suit to match his effortlessly tousled hair and exquisite blue eyes. He grinned when he saw her, but she saw an undertone of anticipation beneath his smile.

"I don't like you in a suit," Lou grinned at him as she climbed out of the car.

"Lou!" Her mother warned through gritted teeth, jabbing her arm.

Hayes chuckled, "I don't like me in a suit either, don't worry about it."

"Where's your father?" Myra asked.

Hayes sighed, "He's inside. Always one for theatrics."

He certainly was.

The inside of the manor was impressive, to say the least. Doors opened to a pearly white grand ballroom. The glossy floor looked up at a chandelier so large that Lou figured that the roof of her own house would cave in if they tried to install it. The room glowed from the tiny, meticulously crafted crystals that reflected golden light onto the walls. Several staircases wound in, out, and around the foyer, leading to spaces unseen onto the floors above. Lou found her eyes trailing up, wanting to see more.

"It-it's like Hogwarts," Lou breathed.

A low chuckle came from behind, and they whirled around.

There stood a man, posture straight and authoritative. His face was aged yet chiseled. From his shiny dress shoes up to his balding, yet still sleek looking hair, Miles Dayholt projected complete high-caliber and serenity. It was terrifying.

"I'm glad you find my home sufficient," his voice was deep and smooth. Lou was sure he could talk a boat into sinking with that voice.

"Dad," Hayes said, breaking up the tension, "This is Lou and her mother Myra."

"No need for redundancies, son. I know who they are."

Hayes shrunk back, very un-Enterprise-y of him. Miles seemed to hold this power over him that was dangerous and unyielding.

Lou straightened, pulling herself up to her full height.

"Thank you for having us, Mr. Dayholt," she tried to smile naturally at him, but could tell it was faker than Miles' own smile back. She was at least pleased that her voice came out clear and confident.

Miles just nodded in reply.

"Well, shall we go?" Hayes said, eager to break up the moment.

"Fine," Miles' honey-sweetened voice fell flat at the request, annoyed to be taking orders from his son. His shoes squeaked on the freshly polished floor as he turned his back to them.

He led them to a balcony that overlooked the Laguna Hills in all of its glory. The sun was already beginning to fall towards the horizon, and a purpled sky cast dim light across the enchanting landscape. The trees danced in the soft breeze. In the distance, Lou could see the yellow lights of other houses. Oh, what a thing, Miles Dayholt's kingdom. The house was his castle, the trees and puny homes that lay nestled below his loyal subjects.

"Have a seat," he said, gesturing to a long, candlelit table. White curtains made from a light fabric blew in towards the balcony, creating an otherworldly effect.

Hayes pulled out a chair for her, and Lou sat down reluctantly. They exchanged a look of unease. She wondered how long it would be before Miles Dayholt would address the elephant in the room, but she didn't mind putting it off. She let a waiter pour fresh spring water in her glass, but she didn't drink. This felt like the kind of event someone would be poisoned at.

Miles sat at the end of the table, looking very domineering in the glow of the candlelight.

"I trust your journey went smoothly?"

Lou wasn't sure if she would call the car ride in a Lamborghini a *journey*, but she submitted.

"Yes, very nice," she said. "Chad is a real treat."

Next to her, Hayes snorted, and Lou found herself biting her lip to prevent herself from doing the same. Myra flashed a warning look from across the table, and Lou fiddled with her napkin.

The meal came in five courses, and the only food she recognized was the salad. She poked at a piece of ambiguous looking meat and scraped oil off of her bread. Her mother shook her head disapprovingly, and Lou stopped inspecting the food. For the majority of the meal, they sat in silence. Only once in a while would someone comment about the deliciousness of the wine or the beauty of the night. Lou and Hayes exchanged silent communication via comforting hand squeezes beneath the tablecloth.

They made it all the way to dessert before the trouble started.

"So, Lou," Miles tapped his face with his napkin, "I am aware that you and my son have been spending quite a lot of time together this summer."

"How'd you know that?" Hayes asked.

"Why, don't you remember? You showed me all of your most recent photographic endeavors!"

Judging from the look on Hayes' face, Lou gathered that he in fact *had not* shown his dad any pictures from the summer.

"There were pictures at the beach, the drive-in, on the hiking trail..."

Hayes bit his tongue. He knew where this was going.

"Speaking of the hiking trail, I noticed that you were photographed with an older man. Do you know what I am talking about?" His eyes bore into Lou's but luckily, she had lots of practice deflecting the stare of a Dayholt.

"No, sir," she said.

"How about I jog your memory," he sniffed daintily and clasped his hands together on the table. "A man with a *red baseball cap,* hm?"

Across from her, Myra lowered her brows.

"I'm sorry, Mr. Dayholt," Lou kept her tone even and light. "I'm afraid I don't know what you are talking about."

Miles' expression remained stony and unyielding.

"Interesting," he said quietly. "Because I recently watched a little documentary—"

"Dad," Hayes gripped his hands on the table, "don't."

"I'm only making conversation, *son*."

"How about we talk about something else, okay?" Hayes flung his napkin off of his lap and onto the table in a manner that betrayed his elegant upbringing.

Miles' expression transitioned from cloudy to full-on stormy.

"No, son. We are going to talk about this."

"Who wants tea?" Myra interjected. "Anyone want tea? I could go for tea."

Miles ignored her.

"I know who you are, Lou Brightly."

"Father!" Hayes jumped to his feet, knocking his chair over. "That's enough!"

"*Sit down,* Hayes!"

Hayes glowered at his father and then flopped back down into his chair.

Lou found herself fidgeting with her bangs.

"I think there must be some kind of misunderstanding," she said shakily.

"No," Miles objected defiantly. "No there is not."

"I think we should get going," Myra said, pushing back her chair.

As if in cue, one of the servants closed the double doors to the balcony. Lou flinched when she heard the *click* of the lock.

Miles smiled cordially, although the redness of his face and the veins popping out in his forehead betrayed his calm expression.

"I believe your only exit is closed, madam." He laughed eerily, "Unless of course anyone would care to jump," he gestured to the balcony, an unhinged look flashed through his eyes before it disappeared as quickly as it came.

Myra scowled at him.

"I swear to you, if you harm one hair on my daughter's head, I won't hesitate to roundhouse kick you in that million-dollar smile. I don't care how rich you are."

"I don't want to harm your daughter," he mused calmly. A waiter brought him a bowl of chilled water and the room watched as he expertly dipped his fingers in before bringing them to his face to pat the droplets gently on his cheeks. "Now look at me, I'm all flushed from this excursion."

He shook his head and surprisingly loosened his tie slightly. "I only want information, Ms. Brightly. I do not want any more games, and I certainly do not wish to be continually provoked." His hand lazily fanned air against his face. If she were to compare this Miles to the one she met at the door, she would have never realized they were the same person. The power and elegance was still there, but now it was tainted with the air of a small child who held their breath and turned purple until they got their way.

"You can't hold us here against our will. I'll call the police!" Lou challenged, not spurred by his looser attitude.

Hayes grumbled through gritted teeth, "He's friends with the police chief."

Myra laughed deep from her chest until it turned into a groan, "Of course he is."

"*Mom*," Lou cautioned.

"At least your daughter has her senses together," he smiled politely, turning to glare at Myra.

Lou started seeing red. She pounded her hands flat against the table and leapt to her feet.

"That's it! Don't talk to my mother like that, asshole." she glowered at him, and the white curtains whipped even more violently in the wind.

"Lou— "

"Shut up, Hayes!" she didn't take her eyes off of Miles, who looked annoyingly collected. "So, you know about me. That's fine. But I also know about *you*."

"Lou!" Hayes and her mother shouted at once.

Her eyes narrowed, "You talk to my mother like that again and I'll— "

Hayes grabbed her arm and pulled her back into her seat.

"What, Hayes?" she hissed.

"Lou, look!" he pointed down the table.

The first thing she saw was a flash of red: a baseball cap.

Clyde Grivins had materialized at the end of the balcony. He did not look happy.

A sudden frost crept up the table and fogged the wine glasses. Miles Dayholt became rigid in his chair, his hand clutched around a steak knife. A breeze blew across the balcony, and the candles winked out.

"Miles Dayholt."

The voice made the hairs on Lou's arm prickle.

"I will get my revenge"

In the darkness, she could only make out Miles' eyes. They were wide with terror.

The last word that hung on Clyde's lips before he evaporated was, *"Soon."*

Then he was gone.

On the balcony, all was silent. Even the mild breeze was nowhere to be found. Four pairs of lungs held their breath as they processed what they had just witnessed.

The only thing Lou could think about was the medium. *Troubled souls. They can do terrible things. Not him. The other one.*

Her heart beat like a metronome in her chest as she looked at Hayes, whose brilliantly blue eyes looked black with panic.

"I will get my revenge."

It all made sense now.

Miles had taken Clyde's life. Why wouldn't Clyde take his son?

For the first time that entire night, Miles Dayholt looked distressed. His menacing eyes were wild. They looked like the eyes of someone who experienced *true, unadulterated fear.*

"Get out of my house!" he cried suddenly. "I never want to see you or your blasted mother ever again!"

Lou and Myra didn't have to be told twice. They jumped out of their seats and bustled out into the foyer. Someone had already unlocked the balcony doors.

Hayes followed close behind.

"Lou!" he called. "Lou, I'm so sorry!"

She glanced back for a fleeting moment, but his suit and sandy hair were only a wet blur.

"Lou!" he shouted again.

"Don't!" She stopped just before the door to the veranda.

"It's okay," he said, grabbing her hand. "Like I said, I'll help you figure this out."

"What is there to figure out? Just by being near you, I'm putting you in danger!"

"But—"

Lou tore her hand away from his grip.

"Did you not see what just happened? He's *dangerous,* Hayes!" A tear rolled off of her cheek and onto the waxy floor. "What kind of person would I be to let you get hurt?"

"But Lou—"

"I'm so sorry," she choked through her tears, "that I was ever selfish enough to think that I could keep you in my life."

She brushed her hands beneath her eyes and burst out into the cool night.

19

FATHER DEAREST

Lou had never been drunk before, but she woke up the next morning in a hangover of sorts. Something soft brushed against her hand, and she opened one eye. At her side was the little girl, whose small, childish hands held her own.

"Good morning," she whispered.

Lou rubbed her forehead. Her head was throbbing, each heartbeat a gentle pulse above her left eyebrow. She groaned and closed her one open eye. When she opened it again, the girl was gone. It was only when Sunny started licking her face that she decided to get up.

Upon looking in the mirror, Lou discovered that she was still wearing most of the night before. Her face was tear streaked. The cherry lipstick had faded and smeared across her cheek. Her under-eyes were swollen from lack of sleep.

She exhaled loudly through her nose.

No matter how terrible she felt, Lou was determined to pick herself up. If she was ever going to survive 'Moving On', she needed to start now.

Sunny looked on as she removed her makeup and brushed the knots out of her hair. A cold shower and some fresh clothes later, Lou realized defeatedly that she didn't feel any less miserable. But at least she no longer looked the part.

She heard stirring in the house. Her mom must have been awake.

"What do you think, Sunny?" she said, stroking her soft ears. "Do we dare leave our room?"

Sunny wagged at the attention and cocked her head confusedly.

Lou sighed. If she wanted coffee, she would have to leave her room.

She hadn't thought that her situation could be any worse. That is, until she stepped across the creaky floorboards to the kitchen, where her mom sat at the breakfast table having friendly conversation with a man.

It only took her a few seconds and some quick calculations to figure out who it was.

It was her father.

"No," she said, throwing her hands up to her head.

Myra and her father cut their conversation short and turned their heads to her.

"Hey kiddo," her father said.

It had been almost ten years since she had seen her dad. The sight of him was an electric shock, a sudden dive into icy water. Looking at him was like looking at an older, taller, male version of herself. Brown hair. Distinct hazel eyes. He smiled.

Lou didn't.

"What is he doing here?" she asked, ignoring him completely.

"Lou Brightly," her mother scolded," where are your manners?"

"Manners?" Lou cackled. "You're the one who was always saying you were glad he left!"

Myra slammed her mug down on the table.

"Excuse me?"

"Myra," her father said, "It's okay, really. It's been ten years. Give her a break."

"No!" Lou shouted. "You—you're not allowed to be on my side. Don't vouch for me now. Where were you when I was seven? You were supposed to protect me!"

He put a hand on the back of his neck, a nervous tick that Lou had long forgotten about. She could bear to forget it again.

"I trusted you!" she yelled, and then she glanced at her mother. "*We* trusted you!"

Myra was on her feet and holding her hands out gently.

"Lou, think about the circumstances we're in. We need help.

If anyone can figure out what's going on with the spirits, it's your father."

"He ruined my life."

"That's a tad bit dramatic, don't you think?" Myra rubbed her forehead.

A realization hit Lou with a violent sting. She looked at her mother.

"*You* called him."

"I did," her mother sighed and nodded.

A million thoughts rushed through Lou's head, the hurt inside growing like a balloon filling up with water. The documentary. The murder. Hayes. And now this. She sniffled.

"Come on, Sunny," she said, grabbing her shoes.

"Where do you think you're going?" Myra asked with her hands on her hips.

"Away. Far away from here." With that, she snatched her mother's car keys, beckoned for Sunny, and slammed the door behind them.

20

CLEO'S STORY

Lou had no idea where she was going, but she kept driving. She rolled down the window for Sunny, who poked her nose out gratefully. It didn't take long for Lou to realize that she had forgotten her phone, but there was no way she was going back to get it. Not a chance.

Why would her mother do such a thing? She couldn't believe it. After years and years of touting that boys were scoundrels and not to be trusted, Lou never expected her mother to let the one who betrayed her the most back on her doorstep. Worse—she had *asked* him to come.

"Can you believe her, Sunny?" she asked.

But Sunny didn't care. She was perfectly content with her head stuck out the window, the wind rippling through her ears.

Where to go. She had hoped to find comfort in the solitude of the drive, but she had not. She wanted someone to talk to. Someone to which she could vent. Someone who would understand. Lou had a dangerous inkling of an idea, but it would be ballsy.

Before she could fully process what she was doing, she found herself engaging her turn signal and winding up Laguna Hills.

• • •

The black gates at Cleo's house were wide open, and strings of fairy lights wrapped around the stucco mansion. Expensive-looking cars were lined all up and down the gravel driveway, and Lou could hear the faint chatter and ringing laughter of people in the distance.

Sunny pressed her nose up to the window and wagged, excited about all of the action.

"What's going on?" She said to herself as she parked her car behind a Buick.

Lou didn't know how rich people felt about dogs, but there was no way she was going to leave Sunny in the hot car. She stayed at Lou's side as she crossed the wide, perfectly tailored lawn. Around the back of the house, fancily dressed people in various states of sobriety milled about. Beneath a large oak tree stood some Harvard-professor types who appeared to be in a deep philosophical conversation that involved a lot of hand gesturing. To the right, a group of young adults were pouring each other drinks at the foot of one of the biggest water fountains Lou had ever seen. She watched amusedly as one particularly inebriated young man with a disheveled tie fell backwards into the pool, the girls shrieking with laughter.

"Didn't expect you here," a soft voice said, close to her ear.

Lou smiled, "Hi Cleo."

She turned to find Model-Boy looking particularly model-y with his patterned silk shirt and curls that kissed his forehead. His brown eyes seemed less boyish tonight, and Lou thought that it may have correlated with the champagne that he held lazily.

"What is the party for?" she asked.

"It's my birthday," he said flatly.

"What? Why didn't you tell me? I would've gotten you something."

Cleo looked back at the bustling activity in his yard and chuckled, "I don't like to make a big deal out of it."

Lou grinned.

"What do you call this?" she asked.

"This? This is really all for my parents," he said, sipping his champagne. "Anyways," he said, lowering his glass, "What are you doing here?"

Lou felt suddenly embarrassed for intruding on his birthday. She blushed.

"Oh. Uh. Nothing," her alarmed voice came out louder than she intended. Her feet started backing away before she could realize it. "I should really just go."

"Lou," he scolded softly. "Don't tell me you came all the way out here to watch some drunk rich folks fall into a water fountain."

Lou stopped, begrudgingly. She never seemed to be able to hide anything from Cleo. She sighed.

"My dad's back."

Cleo, who had just taken a fresh ship of champagne, quickly spit it out into the grass.

"What? Why? What's he doing here?"

"My mom called him."

"*What?* Oh..." he trailed off.

"I assume Hayes told you about last night."

"Yeah," he answered apologetically with a sheepish smile.

The two of them stood side by side in silence, staring out at the party. Lou enjoyed this moment. The togetherness. Being understood. Looking on at a world that didn't stop.

Then Cleo remarked, "Look, I know it's hard. But I think that you're doing the right thing."

She jolted.

"What?"

"I just mean," he started defensively, "that you're protecting Hayes. You left before he could get hurt too badly."

Lou didn't know if Cleo meant *hurt* in the literal sense or the emotional sense. It didn't matter. Somehow, hearing it from someone besides herself stung.

"How can you say that?"

Cleo reared on her.

"I thought that's what you wanted to hear. Isn't that what everyone wants to hear? That they're doing the right thing?" He tipped the rest of his champagne out onto the grass and threw the glass away thoughtlessly.

"You don't understand," Lou urged, "I *love* him."

"Well stop loving him!" In an instant, it was clear that Cleo regretted the words that flew from his lips. But Lou wasn't going to give him a break.

"Are you serious? He's your best friend! Are you really going to justify a wrench between me and Hayes because of *jealousy?*"

He grinned wildly, but it was anything but friendly, "Wow, you're really a lot fuller of yourself than you let on."

Lou shook her head in disbelief.

"You're drunk. And I'm leaving. Come on, Sunny!" She called to her dog who had found her way into the water fountain, splashing about and shaking herself dry at the expense of the party-goers' clothes.

"Wait, Lou!" he groaned, stumbling across the lawn to catch up to her.

She kept on marching, Sunny happily trotted along under the impression that they were going for a walk.

"I'm sorry, Lou!" he called.

She whirled around to face him.

"I knew I was going to lose Hayes, but I didn't think I was going to lose you, too," she seethed at the young man pleading back at her.

"You're not losing anyone!" Cleo grabbed her arm, to stop her from walking away again. "We'll figure this out. Maybe your dad will have answers. Maybe—"

"No!" she screeched and party-goers turned to watch the drama unfold like a bad soap opera. "I can't do this anymore." Her eyes narrowed. "It's like you said. Best to leave before anyone gets hurt too badly." She yanked her arm away.

"You don't think I'm already hurt?" he yelled. "I love you, Lou!"

She stopped dead in her tracks once more. The three words had stunned her, making the world incomprehensible. *Not him. The other one.*

But that wasn't fair. It would *never* be fair.

"I'm sorry," she breathed, not daring to look back at the deep brown eyes of the boy who had just opened his heart to her.

• • •

This was the first time Cleo Allegretti had been in love. He had had a love *interest,* but it had ended rather disappointingly.

When Cleo first met Hayes, he was fifteen and had just moved to Orange County from Italy. Quite the culture shock, to say the least. Within his new neighborhood of old money and continuous wealth, there was only one friendly face: the face of Hayes Dayholt, who was welcoming to all and played by his own rules.

As soon as the jet lag wore off, Cleo and Hayes were an inseparable duo. Cleo was the new kid in town and Hayes, before Cleo arrived, had been the *only* kid in town—besides his older brother Robert, but Robert was, well, Robert.

They were constantly out on adventures, boating, trekking up Laguna Hills, and taking pictures for Hayes' ever-evolving portfolio. Cleo had even been there the day Hayes rolled up with his brand-new shiny stick-shift BMW, a purchase which greatly annoyed Hayes' father, but Cleo knew that was why he had gotten it.

It was around that time when he met Aria.

The boys ran into her at the beach one day, and Cleo was instantly infatuated by her long, dark hair and contagious smile. She started hanging out with the boys more frequently, and they showed up on the shoreline of Laguna Beach at the same time nearly every day.

A week or so in, Cleo planned to make his move, only to find out that she was, in fact, interested in Hayes.

Hayes, being the loyal, chivalrous type, said no.

A few days and some Italian soap operas later, Cleo had picked himself up and moved on from Aria and her long, silky hair. But Lou was different. With Aria, he had been infatuated. Cleo knew he wasn't infatuated. Something about watching Lou walk away with her back to him felt worse than any pain he had ever felt.

This had to be love.

And it was because he loved her that he wouldn't stop fighting. Not until she was happy.

21

TO KILL A GHOST

hen Lou returned home, she found Myra and her father sitting idly in their chairs at the table. It was as if they hadn't moved all day. The only difference was a pile of dishes that had accumulated, and the scowl with which she was met.

"Hello, Lou," her mother said tartly. "Come back to yell at us some more?"

She looked shamefully at her black converse.

"I'm sorry."

"I'm not the one who needs the apology," Myra said, gesturing with her head at her father.

"I'm sorry, Dad," Lou mumbled.

"You don't need to do that," her dad said. He sat hunched over, eyes downcast across the table. He ran his fingers along the grains of the wood. "I've made many mistakes in my life. But jeopardizing my relationship with you is my biggest regret. *I'm* sorry."

Lou sniffed.

"Call it even?" she said, although she knew it was definitely *not* even. Not even close.

Her father chuckled, "Sure kid."

They shook on it, and Myra rolled her eyes.

"You two," she said playfully.

Lou was startled. It had been a long time since she and her father had been "you two." She slipped her hand away warily.

"Anyway," Myra said, eager to break the moment of tension, "while you were gone, doing God knows what," she said, still irritated, "we were here discussing our master plan."

"Not a master plan," her father corrected. "Just an idea."

"A possible solution," Myra said, looking to Lou's father for confirmation. He nodded.

Lou perked up at this.

"A solution? A real solution?"

"Well," her father rubbed his chin, "we don't know yet."

"David," her mother admonished, "let's try to be optimistic." She pressed a rose healing crystal into his palm, something that would have started a long argument ten years ago. David did not believe nor approve of 'spiritual who-haw,' as he called it. But he sat up straight in his chair and tolerated it.

"Alright," he relented. "I think that I may have made a breakthrough in my research in the past couple of months. I've been focusing on exorcism, you see. I think that it might be possible that we can, in a word, 'kill' Clyde's ghost."

"But isn't exorcism when you are trying to get a ghost *out* of something? Like a person's house?" Lou asked. "Clyde isn't inside of me, possessing me or anything. He's his own independent thing...I just happen to be able to see him."

"That's what I said," Myra chimed in.

"Yes, but I think that we can still harness the basic tools of exorcism." He leaned across the table and stretched into full professor form. "Ghosts can use the energy of one's aura to manipulate the space around them. If you have an especially strong aura, like yourself," he winked at Lou, "you may even be able to see them. You knew that, right?"

"Yep," she said, thinking back to the medium.

"I didn't know that." Myra said, looking at Lou. "How'd you know that?"

"Never mind," Lou said. "Keep going."

"Using a series of combustion-based chemical reactions, we may be able to rearrange the autonomy of the energy to eliminate the source of Clyde's stamina!" David sat back in his chair proudly, as if he had just delivered the punch line to a fantastic joke.

Lou and Myra blinked at him.

He sighed, "We can close the gateway that allows Clyde to do all of his spooky stuff. And it will involve fire."

"Fire!" Myra and Lou exclaimed together.

"I did not sign up to be roasted alive," Lou replied flatly.

"It would be a controlled fire," he amended.

"But why fire? Does that actually do anything?"

"Why do you think all seances have candles?"

Lou had to admit—he had a point.

"Okay," she started, "what then? What's the catch?"

"There is no catch," David said. "Once we perform the exorcism, you shouldn't see ghosts ever again."

"What?" Lou recoiled. "None? Ever again?"

"That's right," he said. "Once we close the gateway, it's not going to open back up."

Lou's voice quivered, "But what if I don't want to say goodbye to them all?"

David smiled sympathetically.

"I know, kiddo. But unless you want the violence to escalate, you've got to make a choice."

As if on cue, the sweet scent of caramel drifted through the air. Out of the corner of her eye, Lou saw the old woman with the crinkled, smiling eyes tilt her head solemnly.

22

WICKED TRADEOFF

"I don't know," Cleo said. "He doesn't look too good."

The boys were sprawled out on the floor of Hayes' bedroom with his laptop. They were determined to pin down Hayes' father, and they thought that researching private investigators on Yelp was a step in the right direction. The man they had pulled up on the screen now was a large, dumpy man with the name Alfred Dupus.

"Come on, Cleo," Hayes groaned. "He's got good reviews, look," he said, scrolling to the bottom of the screen.

"I can't believe you think Yelp is a good resource."

"People are honest on Yelp," Hayes shrugged.

"If my name was Dupus, I'd be smart enough to get it changed."

"What are you talking about? Dupus is a fine name."

They snickered.

When Cleo showed up at Hayes' house ready to solve the shit storm that had become their existence, the two brokenhearted boys had perked up dramatically. There's something dreadful about being miserable alone, but something healing about being miserable alongside someone else.

"Shall we give him a call?" Hayes asked.

"Put him on speaker," Cleo grinned.

• • •

Alfred Dupus' chin was falling closer and closer to his chest every second in passing when the shrill nose of the telephone woke him with a start.

119

"Wha-a?"

His hands fumbled over the receiver, and he picked up the call.

"Alfred Dupus, private investigation services, how can I help you?" he said in his trained monotone greeting.

A young voice spoke strong and clear at the other end of the line.

"Good afternoon, Mr. Dupus. I am looking to initiate a private investigation concerning my father."

Alfred picked crumbs from his wrinkled button-down.

"Alright," he cleared his throat, "what is the crime in which you have probable cause to believe your father committed?"

"Murder," the voice said casually.

Dupus straightened.

"Murder? That is quite an accusation, young man."

"Like you said, I have probable cause." Alfred thought he heard another voice laughing in the background.

He grunted.

"Alright, then." He fished a pen out of his pocket. "What is your name?"

"Hayes."

"How do you spell that?"

"H-A-Y-E-S."

Alfred scribbled it on a sticky note.

"What is your father's full name?"

"Miles Richard Dayholt" he answered coolly.

Alfred dropped his pen.

"I'm sorry, I think I misheard you, sir. Can you please say that again?"

"Sure. Miles Richard Dayholt."

Dupus tilted in his swivel chair, clambering to the hard floor. He tried to catch the phone, bouncing it from hand to hand. He snatched the receiver sloppily.

"Uh...Mr. Dupus?"

"Yes!" he answered a bit too loudly.

"You okay?"

"Fine," he brushed off concern he was sure the boy was faking, setting his swivel chair upright, "Just going through some filing cabinets here."

"Okay...is there any more information you need from me?" This time Alfred did hear a laugh but chose to ignore it.

"Actually, I believe that is quite enough," Alfred could barely contain his fear and just wanted to be rid of this unnerving young man.

"Are you sure?"

"Yes," he huffed. "In fact, someone else has already asked me to investigate your father. I just hadn't expected his own *son* to call in."

"Really?" the voice sounded surprised. "Can I ask for their name?"

"I'm afraid not. Confidential," he explained.

"Oh. I see. Well can you tell me what you were investigating him for?"

Dupus sighed.

"Normally I wouldn't do this...it's against protocol...but seeing as you're his son...I've been looking into the connection between your father and the murder of Clyde Grivins."

"The murder in Bali?" the voice said urgently

"That's the one."

"Did you find anything out?"

"Yes," Dupus heaved himself back into his chair. "I believe that your father has been successful at perpetrating several corporations over the past few years.

"I'm sorry, sir. I'm afraid I don't know what that means."

"Your father is a con-artist."

"Oh." The voice sounded disappointed, but not very surprised. "Yeah, everybody knows that. Go on."

This startled Alfred and he cleared his throat before continuing, "As I was saying, your father was very successful until Clyde Grivins came along."

"What happened?" The young man was pushy, but he sounded afraid. Either of his father or of the truth.

"Clyde was quite skilled himself when it came to hustling. Unfortunately, surveillance footage shows that he and your father crossed paths in Bali. They both wanted the same thing. But they also didn't want each other to have it. Somehow—I'm not sure how—but Clyde knew about your identity."

"What? Mine?" The young man's voice grew louder. The other voice in the background gasped and whispered "*what?*" close to the receiver.

"I'm afraid so," Alfred cleared his throat again, trying to not sound as uncomfortable as he felt, "Clyde bartered your life for the money."

"Shit!" The young Hayes yelled, and the other voice whispered an almost indistinguishable "*what the fuck, dude.*"

"Yes," Dupus said cautiously. "Luckily, your father chose to walk away in order to save you."

"Wow. I feel so special," the boy flat-lined sardonically. "So how did Clyde end up dead?"

Alfred Dupus chose his words very carefully. "Well. Even though the footage shows your father walking away, I can imagine your father was thinking, *why can't I have both?* How could he get the money *and* save his son's life? Well, here's our answer: nine hours later, Clyde was found dead, and the money was gone."

23

MIDNIGHT REVELATION

Miles Dayholt hated hotel rooms. Yet, once again, he found himself in one. After the events of the night before, he had thrown some clothes into a suitcase and checked himself into a crappy local hotel called *The Morning Dove*.

He marveled at how bad his circumstances must be for him to stoop so low.

It was the start of his second sleepless night. He lay beneath cool white sheets that reminded him of sandpaper. He curled his toes in a lousy attempt to retain heat. The broken air conditioning had the room boiling only an hour before, but now Miles couldn't stay warm.

By the door, he heard a faint clicking noise.

"Do not disturb," Miles called out. In a hotel like this, he would expect nothing less than to find the staff hauling a vacuum up the stairs to clean his room in the dead of night.

He waited for the footsteps of the maid to recede, but he didn't. Thinking about it now, Miles didn't think he had heard *any* footsteps. He straightened in his bed, which groaned beneath him.

"Hello?" he said, feeling very silly for submitting to such unfounded terror.

There was no answer.

Sheepishly, Miles threw his legs over the side of the bed and stuffed his feet into some slippers. He tightened his bathrobe around him, rubbing the circulation back into his arms. He stepped across the synthetic blue carpeting and extended his arm to turn on the lamp. Just as he did so, the lamp tipped off the table and plummeted to the carpet.

He hadn't touched it.

"Hello?" he repeated, as if that would somehow remedy the situation.

For a while, nothing happened, and he stood in the darkness with bated breath.

Suddenly, instead of clicking at the hotel door, he heard *scratching*.

Oftentimes people look back at their life and pick out moments that they feel defined them. This was one of those moments for Miles Richard Dayholt.

His body went rigid. His face went white. It was as if he was in one of those dreams where he tried to run but his legs had turned to glue.

The door had swung open so far that it hit the wall behind it. The dim light of the hotel hallway cast a halo around a man with a red cap, clear and tangible. Clyde Grivins was red with fury.

"Tomorrow," he said. *"Tomorrow the girl I am drawing my energy from will fill my tank's capacity. Then I will do what I have promised."* His eyes glowed like cat's.

"C—Clyde—" Miles couldn't contain the fear in his voice.

The door flew shut, Clyde disappearing just as quickly as he had come.

Miles shook, but he was left with an epiphany.

The girl! he thought. *Of course! That's the source of his power!*

He froze in place. The room felt warmer. He smiled.

Miles Dayholt had just come up with an abominable solution.

24

VISITOR

Lou was alone. Utterly alone. Both of her parents had left the house for coffee. She had pointed out that there was plenty of coffee in the house, but the resistance in her mother's eyes told her all she needed to know. They wanted to be alone.

Even Lou's ghosts were nowhere to be seen. The last she had seen of them was the old woman, right after her father told her that in a few short days, she would be saying goodbye to them altogether. It was funny. She had never missed her ghosts before. But all of a sudden, the world felt very empty. There were a dozen holes in Lou's heart. Two of them were for Cleo and Hayes, but she vowed to herself that she wasn't going to think about them. Not now. For now, she preferred the numbness.

She heard Sunny growl in the other room. Historically, Sunny was not a vicious dog, but here she was, front legs perched on the windowsill, growling low and aggressively. Even the fur along her back spiked in a defensive manner.

"What?" she said, looking out the window.

There was an overgrown shrub of sorts that always tickled Lou's bedroom window, so it took a while for the wind to blow the branches out of the way before she could get a clear view of their driveway. A red Ferrari snaked down the slope and parked just before the front door.

She frowned. Unless Hayes or Cleo had gotten a new car, she didn't recognize it. But then again, who else with a red Ferrari would choose to stop at a little yellow house hidden behind a concrete hill?

"Relax Sunny," she said, marching to the front door. She thought about what could possibly be so important that they felt the need to drive all the way here just to say it. In her mind, she had been clear about her wishes. Lou wanted more than anything to forget the boys she met that summer.

She exhaled loudly through her nose and swung the door open. Her face fell.

It wasn't Hayes. Or Cleo. It was Mr. Dayholt.

He stood on the front porch looking rather wary with his unkempt hair, faded clothes, and dark circles beneath his eyes. He looked completely different from the suave, unyielding man she had seen only a few days prior.

Why is he here? He can't possibly be here to apologize for a few nights ago.

"Can I help you?" she asked, not very politely. Sunny peeked out from behind her legs, teeth baring.

Miles' gaze shifted from Sunny to Lou.

"Are your parents' home?"

What do I say? she thought. This felt like one of those exercises she was forced to do in grade school about answering the door for strangers. The appropriate response always seemed to be "my mom's in the bathtub," or "my dad is in the back loading his rifle."

She settled on, "What's it to you?"

Miles' expression was unreadable. He stepped inside, pushing past Lou.

"Come in, *please*" she rolled her eyes, keeping the door slightly ajar.

Sunny remained glued to Lou's legs, head low and on guard. She barked, one shrill *woof!*

"Please, get your dog under control, will you?" he glowered at her and then at Sunny. Miles had stopped in the middle of the living room with his back to her. His hands were in his pockets.

Only one word flashed behind her eyes. *Murderer. Murderer. Murderer.*

"Look," Lou said, trying to think of a way to get him to leave,

SHE WALKS WITH SHADOWS

"We're having someone come spray for cockroaches any minute now, so why don't you—"

In one swift motion, Miles pulled out a gun and directed the barrel at Lou.

25

TO CATCH A BAD MAN

The sun reflected off of the black pavement, radiating heat onto Cleo and Hayes who stood beneath the veranda at the Dayholt manor. Hayes checked his phone. 12:30. The P.I. should arrive any second.

He didn't take Alfred Dupus to be a Prius man, much less an electric blue Prius man, and yet there he was, pulling up in one.

Dupus had to stoop significantly in order to haul his tall, bulging body out of the car.

"Hello, boys," he said. "Which one of you is young Hayes?"

Hayes held up a hand.

"Ah," Dupus said, stepping forward to shake his hand. "Is your father in the house?"

"No," he said, "two nights ago he checked into a hotel."

Alfred squinted confusedly.

"Why would he do that?"

Cleo and Hayes looked at each other and shrugged.

"He thinks he's being haunted by Clyde's ghost," Hayes said.

Dupus laughed, low and heartily.

"That's crazy."

"Yeah," Cleo breathed, "*totally* crazy." He smiled at Hayes.

"Do you know anything else about my father?" Hayes asked eagerly. "About the murder?"

Alfred straightened in a very business-y way that did not suit him.

"There is new evidence, yes."

Hayes' eyes widened like a small child's.

"Cool! What is it?"

Alfred raised a quizzical brow.

Hayes cleared his throat, struggling to make himself appear less excited about possibly convicting his father.

"Let me guess—classified?" Cleo tried.

Dupus nodded, "Just procedure, boys, nothing personal. You wouldn't believe how many times the relatives of suspects try to manipulate the evidence for the suspect's benefit. I've dealt with too many last-minute alibis and red herrings in my time. It's my job to keep the lid sealed tight on all the evidence."

Hayes smiled weakly, wondering if Alfred remembered relaying all of the information about the surveillance footage over the phone.

"I'll keep that in mind," Hayes grinned a dazzling smile.

Alfred puffed his chest out.

"The next step would be to ask your father some questions of my own. Now, let's see about that hotel."

• • •

Cleo and Hayes sat cramped up in Dupus' Prius in the trashy parking lot of the *Morning Dove Hotel*. Alfred had gone inside to gauge Miles' whereabouts, or at least, his had-been abouts. In a few short minutes he returned to inform the boys that the receptionist had told him that the hotel was empty: the last man had checked out at noon.

"Huh, looks like we just missed him," Hayes said.

"Is there anywhere else your father goes regularly?"

"Here? No. Unless you count our house."

"Well," Dupus grunted as he climbed back into the car, "our next best guess is to head back there."

Cleo gritted his teeth to stop himself from groaning.

"Just trust the process," Hayes hissed in his ear.

But back at the house, there was still an empty space in the garage where Miles kept his Ferrari.

"This is interesting," Alfred sniffed. "Are you absolutely positive that your father had no idea of my coming?"

"I'm positive!" Hayes insisted, throwing his hands up to his head. "He would have had to tap into my phone call from his hotel room at the *Morning Dove*. My dad is crafty but not *that* crafty. "

A door slammed and Robert came sauntering out into the garage.

The three of them froze like small children caught with their hands in the cookie jar.

"What the hell is going on here?" his eyes landed on Dupus. "Who the hell are you?"

"Private Investigator Alfred Dupus at your service," he said.

Robert's gaze shifted to his brother.

"Hayes," he said calmly, "why is there a private investigator in the garage?"

"Just don't worry about it!" Hayes gnarled.

Robert laughed coldly, "Are you kidding me? I am the *adult* here."

Dupus cleared his throat, but Robert didn't notice.

"What did you do?" Robert demanded.

"Nothing!"

"Hayes, buck up and tell me!"

"God, why do you *always* have to be so annoying?" Hayes *hated* acting like a small child, but Robert always brought out that side of him.

"If you don't tell me what this is about right now, I swear I'll tell that girlfriend of yours that—"

Hayes' eyes widened as he was hit with a frightening realization

"Lou!" he said, leaping into the seat of his convertible before anyone could ask what this was about.

Cleo understood immediately, and he flung the passenger door open,

"What is happening?" Robert shouted over the engine, which had roared to life.

Dupus blundered with the door handle, assuming that this must be pretty important. Private investigators are specially trained to recognize when something is important.

The tires screeched as the convertible shot out of the garage, and the engine stalled.

"Damn you, stick shift!" Hayes fumbled with the gears.

While his brother was sorting out his car, Robert slipped into the backseat next to Alfred.

"No!" Hayes said, when he noticed his brother in the rearview mirror.

"Bite me!" Robert said.

"Why do you always have to—"

Before Hayes could finish his sentence, the engine popped, and the BMW squealed down the drive.

26

EYE OF DEATH

Lou now knew what it felt like to be stared down by death. Time froze, and for a moment, the only material things in existence were herself, the dark eye of the gun, and the finger that was perched on the trigger. She often wondered how her ghosts had died, but she never had the gumption to ask. Had they all felt this way in their final moments? Had they too felt time stop? Did they hear the world whisper *this is it?*

She closed her eyes.

She heard a noise that sounded like a growl from a violent beast, and she opened her eyes to see that Sunny had clamped her mouth shut around Dayholt's leg. Miles wailed with pain as Sunny snarled, sinking her teeth deeper and deeper into his leg. The gun clattered to the floor.

Adrenaline hit Lou with one striking rush, and she kicked the gun, sending it ricocheting down the hallway.

The pain was too severe, and Miles was fading. He fell to his knees, hands slapping against the floor. Before she could talk herself out of it, Lou jabbed him in the face with her knee with all of the force and rage her small body could muster. He groaned and slumped to the ground.

Lou sank to the floor, shaking with the thought that just thirty seconds ago, she should've been dead. Sunny rushed over to her, sticking her large nose into Lou's face as if to say *Did you see that?*

"Yes, Sunny," Lou cried, cupping her dog's soft face with her hands. "You saved me!"

Sunny whined happily and went in to lick her face.

Lou recoiled.

"Not after what you had in your mouth," her laugh quivered.

The front door swung open so hard that it cracked against the wall behind it. In came running Cleo, Hayes, and a man Lou didn't recognize.

Hayes' eyes landed on his father, who lay on the floor with his leg a bloody, mangled mess, and then shifted to the gun, which was still spinning on the floorboards halfway down the hallway.

"Holy shit!" he jumped over his father and knelt beside Lou who was still sitting with Sunny. "Lou, are you hurt?"

"No," she grinned, relieved at their arrival, "Sunny protected me."

Sunny wagged at Hayes, the fur around her mouth slightly reddened.

The man Lou didn't recognize knelt to pick up the gun with a handkerchief.

"Did this man try and shoot you, honey?" he asked.

Lou nodded, and Hayes turned white.

"Some dog you got there," he chuckled. "It was good you had 'em here."

Sunny, who seemed to know she was being praised, thumped her tail against the chair behind her.

In front of the door, Cleo seemed to be blocking a fourth party member from coming in.

"Dammit, Cleo, move!" came a voice, which Lou recognized to be Robert's.

"Go back to the car, Robert!" Hayes called.

But it was too late. Robert shoved Cleo aside and his eyes seemed to jump out of his face.

"What the fu—"

"I thought you weren't going to let him in!" Hayes yelled.

"I tried," Cleo said annoyedly, rubbing his arm where Robert had smacked him.

"Would everyone just calm down?" the large man said.

"Calm down?" Robert snorted. *"Calm down?"*

"Where are your parents?" The man asked. Lou presumed him to be a detective or policeman of sorts. He had an air of authority, but not necessarily one of power.

"I'm not sure. They said they were getting coffee, but—"

As if on cue, David and Myra stepped through the threshold, David holding a giant propane tank and Myra a fire extinguisher. They paused mid-step when they saw Miles on the floor and dropped their items ashamedly when their gaze traveled over to the detective.

"Lou! Are you alright?" Myra asked, unable to peel her eyes away from the detective.

"Fine...why do you have a fire extinguisher?"

"Not now, Lou," she said, waving a hand in her general direction. "Who are you?" she said to the round man.

"Private Investigator Alfred Dupus," he held up a badge.

David made a weird noise in the back of his throat, and Myra elbowed him.

"It appears that we may be witnessing the aftermath of a murder attempt," he said.

Myra shrieked; eyes wide with horror.

"What?" Robert stumbled over to the wall to hold himself up.

"Did—did that man there," Myra said pointing to Miles, who laid limp on the floor, "try to kill my daughter?"

"I'm afraid so," Dupus said, holding up the gun in the handkerchief. "But it looks like your dog here did a fine job protecting your daughter," he chuckled.

"Forgive me if I don't laugh," Myra made a face at the laughing detective and knelt to pet Sunny's head between intervals of "What a good, good, *goody, good* girl!"

"If you don't mind," Alfred rolled his shoulders, "I'm going to call in some backup, and we'll get this thing wrapped u—"

Everything darkened.

Sunlight had shone through the windows only moments before, but now it was as if a giant beast loomed over the house, casting a black shadow through the windows. A chilled breeze swept across the room, and Lou recognized the foul smell from the night the old woman had come to warn her.

"What's happening?" Robert asked, looking from Lou to Hayes.

The sound of glass breaking sounded in the kitchen, making everyone jump.

"What is going on?" Robert repeated, this time directing his question at Lou. He advanced on her. "What are you doing? Make it stop!"

"I'm not doing anything!" she screamed, backing up against the kitchen table.

"Robert, knock it off," Hayes warned, grabbing his arm. "She isn't doing anything."

"Shove off, Hayes," he said, pushing past him. "What are you doing, *ghost girl?*"

"Strengthening me," came a low, haunting voice.

Several heads wandered the room, trying to locate the source of the noise, but it came from *everywhere.*

Miles stirred from where he lay on the floor, and his eyes snapped wide open. They rolled around in his head for a moment, like a man possessed before he rasped, *"He's here"*

27

ART OF POSSESSION

It was as if Miles was supported only by puppet strings. His back curved at an obscure angle. His legs jolted to life, kicking and flailing awkwardly. It was only when he managed to stand, jerking and shaking with every staccato movement that they saw his eyes: two black, empty orbs.

"Hello," Clyde said through Miles' mouth.

"Holy shit," Robert breathed.

Everyone in the tiny house squeezed up against the nearest wall, putting as much distance between themselves and the anomaly in front of them.

"Possession," David breathed. "How—"

"She did it," Clyde pointed one long, trembling finger at Lou.

"I didn't do anything!" she cried.

"Why, of course you did," he sneered, *"You've given me life."* He jostled about inside Miles, as if someone was fighting back to the front.

"Everyone get back," David said, fumbling for some matches in his pocket. "We're about to light this place up."

"That won't work!" Myra said, "You said it yourself!"

"We have to do something!" he cried, spilling matches all over the floor.

"I thought you knew what you were doing!"

"I *don't,* alright, Myra, I don't." David gave up and let the matches fall altogether. "The only way to break the gateway—that I can be sure of—is if the person who is being possessed dies."

"You lied to me, you bastard!" Myra gawked at David while the rest of the house watched on in horror and mild fascination.

"I just," David struggled to find the right words, "I wanted another chance!"

"Ugh!" Myra grumbled. "This is so typical of you. I *knew* I should never have called you, I just *knew*—"

"Guys!" Lou pointed to the center of the room.

Miles had once again straightened. Eyes closed, he adjusted his tie serenely. He opened his eyes: two inky black pearls. He snaked his hand up to his breast pocket, where he produced a knife.

"At long last," Clyde inhaled sharply, *"Sweet revenge."*

He lunged at Hayes.

"No!" Lou screamed as Clyde shot forward when—

A wrinkled hand shot through the air, striking Mile's nose with such force that it made an audible *cracking* noise. The scent of caramel hung in the air. Lou's gaze followed the arm back to the old woman, who stood triumphantly in front of Hayes.

"Holy shit!" Robert screamed, walking a circle around himself. "Who is she?"

Clyde stumbled back, barely managing to catch himself with his hands.

Dupus drew his gun.

"Stop!" Hayes yelled. "That's my dad!"

"No it's not, son," Alfred said.

"Yes, it really is!" Hayes pointed. "Look!"

Miles held up his head warily, his two blue eyes muddled with confusion.

"Then where—"

There was a rustling noise, and Robert knelt to pick up the knife that Miles had dropped during his fall.

Lou looked back at Hayes. The old woman in front of him had disappeared.

"I like this body," Clyde flexed Robert's muscles, *"So young. So strong."*

Dupus readjusted his aim.

"Don't shoot him!" Myra said, tilting his gun to the floor. "He's just a kid!"

Robert started to move towards Hayes.

Lou jumped in front of him.

"Lou!" she heard Myra call, "Get your ass out of there *right now!*"

Lou held her ground, but Hayes wasn't having any of it.

"I'm not worth it, Lou! I'm not worth it." His voice gave way to tears as his arms moved up to shove far from him.

"Yes, you are!" she wacked his arms out of her way. "How could you say that?"

"Lou!" She heard her father call.

Robert stopped. He ducked his head, reverting to that same jostled expression as before.

"He's fighting it!" David said, astonished.

"Of course he is!" Hayes laughed, relieving all of the tension he held tight in his chest. "Stubbornness runs in the family!"

"Guys— "Robert's voice broke forth amidst his shifts in control. "What—*ugh*—is—*ugh*—happening?" As horrifying as it was to watch the two men being possessed, it was more horrifying to watch Robert and Clyde struggle for control. Robert's body moved and jolted in positions the human body had no business shifting in. The grotesque facial expressions combined with joints and ligaments twisting in awkward ways made for a terrifying spectacle. Finally, his body released somewhat as he bent over, groaning as he clutched his ribs.

"He's suffering," Dupus said, raising his gun. "We have to—"

"Don't you dare shoot my son!" a voice boomed, and Miles clambered to his feet, blocking Alfred's line of fire. "I may just be an old con-man, but I'm not going to let either of my sons pay for my deeds"

Lou jumped when she saw a flash of warm light burst from the corner. David had lit a match, and he knelt to light one of Myra's candles.

"What are you doing?" Dupus asked.

"Controlling the situation," David whispered back. "Or at least, trying to."

"Good job," Miles rolled his eyes.

"Can it, jackass," Mya snapped. "Don't get all high and mighty with my ex-husband. You still tried to kill my daughter."

"Would it work?"

Half a dozen heads spun towards Lou.

"What?" Myra asked, but she knew where this was going.

"If I died," Lou swallowed, "would this stop?"

"Don't you even dare!" Myra bellowed. "Of course it wouldn't."

Robert jolted for a final time and fell to his knees. A line of sweat broke across his forehead. His eyes focused back into the room.

"Son?" Miles asked, kneeling to his level.

"I'm fine," Robert gasped.

The only noise in the room was the faint crackling of the candle as they waited for Clyde's next victim. Lou looked at her mother. Her father. Sunny, who whined beneath the kitchen table. Cleo with his boyish eyes and sweet smile. Hayes. Charming Mr. Enterprise, who had given Lou her first kiss. All of the people she loved so deeply were in this room. She wouldn't let them get hurt. Not for her.

She turned her attention back to the middle of the room. On the ground, she could make out the sliver, glinting light of the knife.

Lou knew what she needed to do.

Across the room, Cleo felt himself thrust backwards into a black space inside of himself as Clyde took possession of his body.

Cleo knew what he needed to do.

28

CLEO'S SACRIFICE

Lou lunged for the knife.

"What are you doing?" She heard someone call, but she didn't look up to see who had said it.

"*Lou, no!*" she heard Hayes scream.

"I have to," she choked, "I'm sorry. I'm so sorry."

She blocked out the noise of her mother's screaming.

Lou gripped the knife with both of her hands and closed her eyes. *The pain will only be temporary,* she told herself. She held the knife out, ready to thrust.

Something knocked into her, and she felt her head buzz with the shock of the force. Hayes grabbed her and yanked the knife out of her hands.

"Stop!" she protested. "Let me do it! I don't want anyone else to get hurt!"

"And you think doing yourself in is going to stop that from happening?" He locked her arms together. He hissed in her ear, "What about the people that love you who you're leaving behind, huh?"

"I just—" She stopped short as Cleo was walking jerkily about, advancing aggressively just as Robert and Miles had when they were possessed.

Lou's stomach plummeted.

Cleo's boyish, rich honey eyes were black.

Hayes flung her out of the way, and her mother caught her arm, pulling her tight against her chest. She wrestled with her mother.

"Oh no you don't," Myra said. "You're staying *right here.*"

"Fight it, Cleo!" she heard Hayes say.

Lou watched with horror as Cleo parted his lips, and Clyde's voice echoed into the room.

"Justice must be served."

"Cleo!" Hayes said, backing up against the wall. "I know you're in there."

"Nice try, young Dayholt."

In a flash, Clyde had his hands pressed tightly against Hayes' neck, lifting him up against the wall.

"No!" Lou screamed, struggled, and she begged for someone, something, *anything* to make the madness stop. She looked around the room. They all sat stunned, eyes wide and mouths gaping. They had all given up. She kicked her legs and swung her arms but Investigator Dupus was now assisting her mother and they Would. Not. Let. Go.

"Miles!" She called out to Mr. Dayholt, who looked as though someone was tearing his heart out of his chest. "Do something!"

He hid his face, his crying audible behind his hands.

"Cl—Cleo," Hayes choked. He was beginning to turn blue. "I b-believe in you."

As if the Lord had answered her prayers, Cleo's grip relaxed, and Hayes slumped to the floor, coughing as he gasped for air. Cleo stumbled, twisting and turning as he flashed in and out from the front. He crashed to his knees, dragging himself across the floor in slow, jerky movements.

Cleo knew what he needed to do.

When his hands fell on the handle of the knife, he heard Lou's breath catch. He looked at her. She was beautiful. Her hazel eyes glowed with candlelight and tears. He smiled, struggling to hold back Clyde who was somewhere inside of him. His entire body burned. He had to be quick. If he was going to do this, he wanted to do it right. He wanted to do it on his own terms. He wanted a win. Just this once.

He wanted to die as himself.

Fuck off, Clyde, he told the back of his head, where it felt as if something was ripping through his skull. *This is the end of the line.*

Before Cleo plunged the knife into his own chest, he whispered two words:

"I'm sorry."

29

GOODBYE

Lou saw the summer flash before her eyes. Sunny in the front seat of the convertible. Mr. Enterprise and Model-Boy in their sunglasses. The hike, where out of the corner of her eye she saw Cleo spill water down the front of his shirt. The beach. The drive-in. The burrito. Confiding in Cleo, and his promise that he would help Lou through her eating disorder. His gift. The oil pastels that sat untouched in their case, too precious to be used. The night he had told her that he loved her, and she couldn't say it back.

And here she sat now with the boy who stole a piece of her heart in her arms, holding on tightly to his last moments.

"Cleo," she whispered, and his eyelids fluttered slightly. "Why?" She cried. "*Why?*"

He muttered something, but Lou could hardly make it out above the sirens that wailed louder and louder as they approached. She thought she could see a glint of red and blue lights.

Hayes crouched next to him, his eyes red and filled with pain.

"You saved me man," Hayes' voice was weak as he touched Cleo's shoulder gently.

Cleo smiled, "Badass," he mumbled.

"That's right," Hayes said, wiping away a tear as discreetly as possible.

Cleo stirred, trying to say something, but it came out slurred and incoherent.

"What is it Cleo?" Lou shook him, desperate to keep him conscious.

He groaned, and Lou could only make out three words.

"Be happy, Lou."

His chest rose. And then it fell, one last time.

Hayes wailed, closing his hands tightly around Cleo's.

Lou broke, and the room turned into a blur of fluttering candle-light and tears.

Cleo's soul had left his body, and the gateway was closing.

Out of the corner of her eye, she saw the old woman, the man with the fishing pole, and the little girl watching on from the candlelight. Something about them was unusually faded, as if they were using their last scraps of strength to be in that room with her, saying goodbye. For the last time, Lou knew that she was the only one who could see them.

Thank you, she thought, smiling gently at the old woman, *for looking out for me.*

It was the first time Lou saw sadness in the old woman's eyes.

For a split second, Lou saw Cleo's soul looming in the glow of the candlelight. She honed in on it, taking in every last moment of *him.* The air smelt like orange blossoms. Cleo looked at her with his deep brown eyes, boyish to the very end. He smiled as a hot tear rolled off of Lou's cheek and onto Cleo's limp body. He nodded at her, as if to say *You know what you need to do.*

Lou bit her lip, tasting the sharp saltiness of her tears.

I can't! she thought.

Cleo kept his eyes locked on hers.

Please, he said. *Let me go.*

The sharp pain of grief clawed its way up into Lou's chest. She looked at him.

Only for you, Cleo.

With one last quivering exhale, Lou closed her eyes and let him go.

30

THE GIRL WHO WALKS
WITH SHADOWS

It always rained at funerals. At least, in movies it did. But on the day of Cleo's funeral, Lou was shocked to pull open her curtains to find sunshine. She should have known. Rain hardly ever came in the middle of a California summer. But something about it felt wrong. The whole thing felt wrong. The whole world should have been mourning with her.

Lou scooted her folding chair as closely as she could to Hayes at the service, which took place outside in the light of a far too sunny day. He snatched her hand and they both ducked their heads, terrified of accidentally catching a glimpse of one of Cleo's relatives who were clad in black.

Sunny whined and laid her head on Lou's legs. Sunny could always tell when something wasn't right. Lou laid a hand on her head. Her mother sniffled next to her, and Lou noticed that her fingers were tightly interlaced with her father's. Despite the constant shouting, arguing, and chaos that had ensued from his most recent visit, it looked as though her parents were patching things up. Lou wasn't sure how she felt about it, but for a few brief moments she saw love in her mother's eyes when she looked at her father, and so long as her mother was happy, she would be happy.

Hayes wasn't so lucky.

His relationship with his father had...complicated, to say the least. After all, he had tried to kill his girlfriend. Miles was arrested by Private Investigator Alfred Dupus with charges of foul play, attempted murder, and illegal means of acquiring money after new evidence surfaced. Apparently, Miles had been a little overly active on his email.

It came time to place flowers on the casket. A long line of tear-stroked faces formed down the aisle. Lou's legs felt like rubber as she joined the line, her hands sweating on the piece of paper in her hands. She held onto it tightly.

She felt responsible. She knew that she shouldn't. She knew it was irrational. And yet, the feeling was there. The fact was, Cleo had given his life so she could live.

The line moved, and she felt the advancing dread of the last goodbye clang against her heart. A thought struck her. Would Cleo want her to feel this way? Would Cleo want her to spend the rest of her life in the painful wheel of guilt and grief? Is that what he had given his life for?

No.

Lou knew what Cleo would want.

She stopped in front of the casket, the rich grains of wood only inches from her fingertips. She unfolded the piece of paper. She found she could work a nice sunset with the oil pastels Cleo had given her. Cleo had had an affinity for sunsets. She folded the paper and held it to her lips before tucking it amongst the arrangement of flowers, letters, and trinkets.

Goodbye, Cleo.

She stepped away from the casket, allowing Hayes to take her place and pay his respects to his comrade, his savior, his friend.

Lou blinked, looking around for the faintest glimmer of a spirit. Nothing.

There had been nothing since that fateful day when Cleo closed the gate between her ghosts and opened the one for her life. For one week, there had been nothing but the sadness that clouded her heart. No more sweet good mornings from the little girl. No more crinkled smiles from the old woman. And what hurt her the most—there was no Cleo, her beloved friend.

Lou looked at Hayes, and then her mother who held on to her father's arm.

There had been no ghosts.
But Lou knew.
She would never walk alone.

THE
END